"Hi! Mind if I sit down?" Chris said in her best "Charlie" voice. By now, her heart was beating so loudly that she was certain everyone in the room could hear it.

"Nope. Have a seat." Scott glanced at Charlie for only a second before turning back to his tuna fish sandwich.

But Chris was not about to let such a golden opportunity slip by. She sat down right opposite him.

Her initial inclination was to be flirtatious.

Whoa—wait a minute! You're not Chris . . . You're Charlie, remember? You've got to act as if you're just one of the guys. And as if Scott Stevens is also just one of the guys.

As she looked into his green eyes and felt her heart melting, she knew that that was going to be anything but easy.

"My name is Charlie. Charlie Pratt . . ."

Fawcett Juniper Books
by Cynthia Blair:

THE BANANA SPLIT AFFAIR

THE HOT FUDGE SUNDAY AFFAIR

MARSHMALLOW MASQUERADE

THE PUMPKIN PRINCIPLE

STARSTRUCK

STRAWBERRY SUMMER

MARSHMALLOW MASQUERADE

Cynthia Blair

FAWCETT JUNIPER • **NEW YORK**

RLI $\dfrac{\text{VL: Grades } 5 + \text{ up}}{\text{IL: Grades } 6 + \text{ up}}$

A Fawcett Juniper Book
Published by Ballantine Books
Copyright © 1987 by Cynthia Blair

Library of Congress Catalog Card Number: 86-91825

ISBN 0-449-70217-0

Manufactured in the United States of America

First Edition: May 1987

One

"Even if I live to be a hundred, I'll never *understand* boys!" declared Christine Pratt with a loud sigh.

Her best friend, Holly Anderson, looked over at her with surprise. "Why, Chris! I always thought you were the world's expert on that subject."

"I did, too," Chris admitted. "That is, until I met up with Scott Stevens."

"Uh-oh," Holly teased her. "Not the captain of Whittington High's basketball team—not to mention the school's number-one heartthrob. What's going on with you and Scott?"

"There's absolutely *nothing* going on with me and Scott," Chris wailed. "Not for lack of trying, either— at least on my part. I've been running through every trick in the book. I go out of my way to run into him 'accidentally'; I talk to him in history class every day. . . . I even offered to help him study for the big test on the Civil War. And I *still* can't get him to notice me!"

The two girls were in the Pratts' kitchen, making hot chocolate. It was late on a Friday night in mid-November, just two weeks before Thanksgiving, and Christine Pratt and her twin sister, Susan, had each invited a friend to sleep over.

The evening had turned into an informal slumber party: four girls staying up till all hours in their bathrobes and slippers, giggling and eating and talking the entire night away. And so it was inevitable that sooner or later the topic of conversation turned to boys.

"And here I was hoping that Scott would invite me to the Homecoming Dance next Saturday night," Chris grumbled as she stirred cocoa and sugar into the saucepan of hot milk on the stove. "But at the rate things are going, I might end up without any date at all!"

"You could always go with Peter Blake," Holly teased her. "I get the distinct impression that he's got a crush on you."

"Oh, no!" Chris groaned. "Not Peter Blake, the number-one nerd of Whittington High! Why, the only thing he ever talks about is bugs!"

"Bugs?"

Chris nodded seriously. "He's a real nut about nature and animals and all that. Haven't you ever heard him go on about how all animals are wonderful, even ugly little bugs?" She shuddered at the thought. "Oh, if only I could get Scott to ask me to that silly dance. . . ."

Holly, usually bubbly, was pensive as she took four white ceramic mugs off the shelf above the kitchen sink. "Hey, I just thought of something. Maybe Scott already has a girlfriend."

"Not a chance. I already checked into that. According to my in-depth research, the only thing that makes Scott Stevens's heart go pitter-patter is basketball." Chris bit her lip and shrugged. "Maybe I'm losing my touch."

"You, Chris? Never!"

"Well, then, maybe I'm just not his type."

As she poured the hot chocolate into the mugs, she said, "Even though I think he's the dreamboat of the century, I'm on the verge of giving up. Writing him off forever. Admitting, once and for all, that Scott and I simply were not meant to be."

"Well, Chris, if it's any consolation, things between Hank and me aren't going all that smoothly, either."

"Hank! Wait a minute. Didn't you two go out just last weekend?"

Holly nodded. She leaned against the kitchen counter and twisted a strand of her long blond hair around one finger. "Yes, we did. We went to the movies together last Saturday night."

"And how did it go?"

"It was great! We both had a terrific time." Thoughtfully, she added, "At least, *I* did. And it seemed like he did, too."

"So what's the problem?"

"The problem is, ever since then he's acted as if we were total strangers!"

"You mean he hasn't called you?"

"Not only hasn't he called me; whenever I see him at school, he acts as if I've got the bubonic *plague* or something!"

Chris shook her head slowly. "Boys! What on earth goes on in their heads? I sure wish I could figure them out!"

3

"Believe me, Chris, if you could, you'd be a millionaire by the time you were eighteen. You could travel around the country, giving lectures to girls just like us!"

"Wouldn't that be wonderful! Finally, we girls would be able to find out what makes boys tick!"

Holly's dreamy smile faded abruptly. "Unfortunately, that's not about to happen. So in the meantime, let's get this hot chocolate upstairs before Susan and Beth come down to see what's taking us so long." She placed all four mugs on a tray, then added spoons and paper napkins. "For now, we'll just have to resort to the one sure-fire cure for the blues."

"What's that?"

Grinning mischievously, Holly replied, "Why, drowning our sorrows in food, of course!"

Chris laughed. "In that case, we might as well go all the way!"

She pulled out a kitchen chair and climbed up to the cabinet above the refrigerator. After rummaging through the boxes and cans that were tucked away up there, she finally came up with a clear plastic bag printed in red and blue. Triumphantly she waved it in the air.

"What's that?" Holly demanded.

"Marshmallows!" cried Chris. "If we're going to 'drown our sorrows,' we might as well do it right! Here, catch!" She tossed the bag to Holly, down below.

"Hey, you two, we were just starting to wonder what happened," said Susan Pratt, Chris's twin sister, once the two cooks reappeared in Chris's bedroom on the second floor. She was sitting on the window seat,

4

lazily scratching the Pratts' pet cat, Jonathan, under the chin.

"That's right," agreed Beth Thompson, Susan's best friend, who was lounging on the bed. "We were afraid you got so thirsty that you ended up drinking all the hot chocolate before we even got a chance to get near it!"

"I wish," moaned Chris. "No, I'm afraid we were busy complaining."

"About what?" Beth asked, cocking her head so that her short black curls bounced.

"What else?" Holly replied. "We were complaining about boys!"

"Gee," Beth returned wistfully. "At least you have something to complain about! I hardly ever go out. I'm so shy that every time I try to talk to a boy, I end up turning red and stuttering. Half the time, I just feel like running away."

"Well, we have a temporary cure, anyway," Chris said. "Four hot chocolates, coming up. With marshmallows!"

"Great!" cried Susan. "Just the thing for a cold winter night."

The girls were silent as they sipped their hot chocolate. Susan, the more thoughtful of the Pratt twins, took advantage of the first quiet moment of the night to look around at the rest of the foursome lounging comfortably in Chris's bedroom.

Holly Anderson, she decided, was a lot like Chris. It seemed fitting that the two of them were best friends, as they had been since junior high school. They were both outgoing and popular, taking part in so many school activities—committees and clubs and anything else that came along—that they could have made good use of a social secretary to keep track of their busy schedules.

Tonight they were even dressed similarly. Chris, with her shoulder-length chestnut-brown hair and dark brown eyes, was wearing a bright pink nightshirt with the faces of the members of one of her favorite rock groups printed in front. And Holly, so different in coloring, with her long blond hair and blue eyes, nevertheless looked as if she were cut from the same mold in the red oversized tee-shirt that she claimed she had talked her older brother, Michael, into giving her.

On the other hand, Susan and her best friend, Beth, were dressed in old-fashioned flannel nightgowns trimmed with lace. Susan's was pale blue, sprigged with tiny white flowers. Beth wore a white one with a pale pink stripe running through it. With her dark, curly hair, she looked like a character in a picture book of fairy tales.

Yes, we certainly do make an odd group! thought Susan. What a strange mixture of seventeen-year-old girls!

What was even more difficult to believe, however, was the fact that Chris and Susan were twins. After all, the two of them were so different. While Chris was an extrovert, Susan was quiet, preferring reading and listening to music and simply daydreaming to planning a school dance or trying out for the cheer-leading team. Her real passion, however, was art. Susan was quite a talented painter, and she hoped to attend art school after high school graduation.

Even though the Pratt girls were so different from each other, they looked exactly the same. After all, they were identical twins. Both had shining chestnut-brown hair, which they wore at shoulder length, and dark brown eyes, high cheekbones, and ski-jump noses.

We certainly don't look like identical twins tonight! thought Susan with amusement. But that was almost always the case. Unless, of course, the twins made a special effort to look that same. And that was something they had done more than once . . . usually in order to play a mischievous prank.

"So are you two having trouble with your social lives?" Susan asked. Now that she had had a chance to enjoy some of the tasty hot chocolate her sister had just prepared, she was eager to return to the discussion that had been abandoned so abruptly in favor of sweeter pastimes.

Chris rolled her eyes dramatically. "When *aren't* I?" she groaned. "This boy-girl thing is never very easy, is it?"

"It's like a big game," Holly joined in. "Trying to guess what a boy really means when he says something, spending hours on the telephone with your girlfriends trying to predict what he's going to do next . . . Really, I get so tired of the whole thing sometimes."

"I know what you mean," Susan agreed. "I wish boys and girls could just be more *direct* with each other. Say what they mean, without worrying about what the other person is thinking."

Beth sighed. "I wonder if what boys and girls want is really so different. I mean, here we are, talking about boys as if they were—I don't know—*Martians* or something!"

"I think you're onto something!" Holly joked. "Finally, we've figured out what the problem is!"

"No, really," Beth went on. "They're human beings, just like us . . . aren't they?"

"Then why is everything always so difficult?" Chris moaned. "Look at us. We're four perfectly nice, normal teenage girls. And yet I'm all in a tizzy because I don't know what's going on with Scott Stevens, Holly's upset because Hank is suddenly giving her the runaround, Beth is convinced that boys are just like girls, but she just admitted that she can't even talk to them, and Susan . . ."

"I'm just as baffled as you are," Susan laughed. Even though she was among her closest friends, girls she felt she could trust one hundred percent, she didn't feel like admitting to the secret crush she'd developed lately on Michael Anderson, Holly's older brother. "You know one thing that's always bothered me? I mean *really* bothered me?"

"What?" asked her twin.

"The fact that girls aren't supposed to telephone boys. It doesn't make any sense. They're allowed to call us, but all we're supposed to do is sit around and wait for them."

"Yeah," Beth agreed somberly. "It's like something out of the Dark Ages, isn't it? This is the twentieth century, after all! But things haven't changed much since my mother was our age. My grandmother, even!"

"And then there's the problem of what to do if a boy *doesn't* call," said Holly. "We end up wasting our time worrying about if we said the wrong thing or if they don't really like us or if we're too tall or too fat or . . . or too *something*!"

"Do you know what we need?" Beth said, suddenly excited. "We need a *spy*. Someone to find out for the female population, once and for all, what boys are all about."

"Gee, what I wouldn't give to be a fly on the wall at Hank's house one afternoon when he had his friends over!" Holly whooped.

"'A fly on the wall'?" Beth was puzzled. "What does that mean?"

"It means she wishes that she could listen to everything the boys we know say when they think they're alone," Susan explained. "You know, without their realizing anyone could hear them."

"Oh, I see." Beth turned to Holly. "Then you could find out what's been going on in Hank's mind all week. Why he hasn't called you."

"Exactly. And I bet we'd hear a lot more! Imagine: If we could do that, we could find out what each and every boy we know is *really* like! What they talk about, how they feel about girls, how they feel about each one of us . . ." Holly was growing more and more excited as she continued to fantasize about her idea. "Just think! Listening in while all the boys we know talk to their friends! It's . . . it's *mind-boggling*!"

"I'll say," Chris agreed, sounding a trifle glum. "Unfortunately, it also happens to be impossible."

The four girls were silent as they thought about Holly's idea. It was, indeed, wonderful. But Chris was right; accomplishing such a feat was something that could never be done.

"Hey, wait a second," Beth said suddenly. "Maybe it's *not* impossible."

"What do you mean, Beth?" Susan blinked.

"Well, you and Chris are so good at pranks. Maybe

one of you could . . . oh, I don't know, hide in one of the lockers in the boys' locker room or something."

"You mean we could eavesdrop." Chris looked over at her twin. "Well, we've certainly tried our hand at pranks before."

"That's for sure!" Susan agreed.

It was true; the adventurous Christine and Susan Pratt had certainly played quite a few tricks in their time, calling upon the fact that the two of them were identical to do all kinds of things that most people could never get away with. The year before, for example, when they were both sixteen, they had traded places, for two whole weeks, so that each girl could learn more about what her twin sister's life was like. They had dubbed that adventure the Banana Split Affair, since Susan bet Chris a banana split that the two of them could never carry it off. In the Hot Fudge Sunday Affair, they had taken turns being Chris in order to share the rewards of being their hometown's honorary "Queen" during a week-long celebration of Whittington's one-hundred-year anniversary, an award that the girls had worked together to earn. That time, they had had no doubts that they could fool everyone, and they celebrated, at the end of the week, with hot fudge sundaes at Fozzy's, Whittington's new ice cream parlor.

Then, during the summer that they nicknamed Strawberry Summer, their being identical also came in quite handy. Their successful history of pranks was bound to catch up with them sooner or later, however, and right before Halloween, while Chris was testing a theory of hers called the Pumpkin Principle, it was the twins who ended up being tricked—in a way that, fortunately, also turned out to be a treat.

10

"I don't know," Susan said, shaking her head. "Sure, Chris and I have played our share of pranks. But what you're talking about sounds a bit too difficult, even for two experts like us."

"I'm afraid I have to agree with Sooz," said Chris. "This time, the fact that we're identical twins can't be of much help."

"Well," said Holly with a loud sigh, "it was a great idea, anyway. And it was fun while it lasted." She took another sip of her hot chocolate. "You know," she said slowly, "the way I look at it, boys are kind of like marshmallows."

"Marshmallows!" Chris shrieked. "Holly Anderson, what on earth are you talking about?"

"Well," her friend said thoughtfully, "they're sweet and they're fun, and they can take something that's already nice, like hot chocolate, and make it even nicer. But when you come right down to it, we really don't know very much about marshmallows at all, do we?"

"That's right!" Susan agreed, laughing. "Like, how come they float? And why don't they dissolve, if all they're made of is sugar? I think Holly's found the perfect way to think of those mysterious creatures. They *are* like marshmallows!"

The four girls laughed at the image that Holly's comment had conjured up in their minds. It was ridiculous, of course, but late at night, with all four girls together, giggling and talking and having a wonderful time, comparing boys with marshmallows seemed like an inspired idea. It was a good joke, something to make them all laugh, even though they were feeling a bit down about their inability to comprehend the puzzle that confronted them every single day: the opposite sex.

As they finished up their hot chocolate and decided to abandon their woefulness for a game of Scrabble, they forgot all about Holly's teasing remark. It never occurred to any of them that their joking conversation was about to launch the most daring, most intriguing, most *delicious* prank of the Pratt twins' mischievous career.

Two

"So, did you girls have fun last night?" asked Mrs. Pratt over lunch the next day.

The four Pratts were sitting at the kitchen table, finishing up their soup and sandwiches, spending some time together before going their separate ways for the rest of the afternoon.

"What *I* want to know is, did you girls get any *sleep* last night?" the girls father teased them. "When I went to bed, just after eleven, I heard an awful lot of giggling coming from Chris's room. And then, when I got up at seven this morning, I *still* heard giggling!"

"Oh, Daddy!" Chris laughed. "What's the use of having your friends sleep over if all you're going to do is *sleep*?"

Mr. Pratt looked at his daughter quizzically. "I suppose there's some logic there," he said. "But I suspect I'd have to be a teenage girl to understand it. And, unfortunately, it's been a long time since I could honestly call myself a teenager. As for being able to understand the female half of the population—"

"There it is again!" Susan interjected, suddenly glancing up from the grilled cheese sandwich she'd been munching.

The other three Pratts looked at her with surprise.

"There's *what* again?" her twin asked.

Susan's dark brown eyes were shining. "What Daddy just said. About his not being able to understand the female half of the population."

"Gee, Susan, I was only teasing."

"But that's exactly what we were talking about last night! Chris and Beth and Holly and me. The fact that *girls* find it impossible to understand *boys*!"

"Aha," said Mr. Pratt. "Now I see. It works both ways, then."

"Oh, I don't know about that." Mrs. Pratt placed her coffee cup in its saucer and patted her husband's arm affectionately. "I feel as if I understand *you* pretty well, and you're a member of the opposite sex."

"That's different," Chris insisted.

"Why is it different?" Mr. Pratt pretended to be offended. "I'm a boy, aren't I? An old one, maybe, but a boy, nevertheless."

"Because," Chris explained impatiently, "you two are *married* to each other. You're supposed to understand each other by now!"

Mrs. Pratt looked at her husband and smiled. "Let's hear it for the institution of marriage."

"Hear, hear!" Mr. Pratt agreed with a grin.

"We were talking about the boys we know at school," Susan explained to her parents.

"Complaining, you mean," Chris said cheerfully. "Oh, Mom, I'm sure you know what we're talking

14

about. Teenage boys are just *impossible* to figure out! And the four of us were just fantasizing about how great it would be if we could . . . well, *spy* on the boys we know, to find out what they're like when there are no girls around. That way, maybe we'd be able to learn more about what makes them tick."

"My dears," Mr. Pratt said, "the battle of the sexes has been going on since time began. I'm afraid we're not about to solve it over lunch." He gathered up his dishes and silverware, pushed back his chair, and stood up. "Now, if you'll excuse me, I've got about ten thousand things to do this afternoon." He deposited his dishes in the sink and was gone.

"I've got a long day ahead of me, too." Mrs. Pratt downed the rest of her coffee and then she, too, hurried away, anxious to get on with her afternoon.

Chris and Susan lingered at the table. Unlike their parents, they were not in the mood to go rushing off on this crisp, sunny November Saturday. Their discussion of the night before, now revived, had put them both in a pensive mood. It was, in fact, almost as if a strange spell had been cast over them.

"Maybe the 'battle of the sexes' has been going on since time began," Chris grumbled. "But that doesn't mean there's anything wrong with wanting to infiltrate behind enemy lines."

Susan reacted with indignation. "Christine Pratt, boys are not our enemies! And there's certainly no 'battle' going on, either. I still maintain that boys and girls are basically the same. We want the same things; we have the same fears and self-doubts. . . . We just can't be open and honest with each other all the time because, well, we're all so convinced that boys and girls are entirely different!"

Chris sighed. Toying with the last crust of her sandwich, she said, "Maybe you're right, Sooz. But it sure doesn't seem that way most of the time."

Suddenly her eyes began to twinkle. "Hey, that was pretty clever of Holly, wasn't it? Comparing boys to marshmallows? Honestly, I don't know how she comes up with these things!"

"Hey, wait a minute. What about us?" Susan challenged her. "Don't forget that you and I have been known to come up with some pretty outrageous ideas, too."

"Well, I just wish we could come up with an idea for a way to find out more about boys."

"You mean something like hiding in the boys' locker room and eavesdropping?"

Chris wrinkled her turned-up nose. "Not very original. Especially for two masters of disguise like us. I mean, last summer you managed to convince the entire town of Whittington that you were me!"

"You've played your share of practical jokes, too, you know. And, I might add, with earth-shattering success." Susan smiled, then became thoughtful. "It *is* a challenge, isn't it? Coming up with some sort of scheme that would help us delve into the secret lives of boys."

"You make it sound so mysterious, Sooz!" Playfully Chris placed a strand of her chestnut-brown hair under her nose, like a mustache. Moving her eyebrows up and down comically, she said in a funny voice, "Vel-come to the see-cret vorld of boys!"

She expected her sister to laugh. Or at least smile. Instead, Susan just stared at her.

"Come on, Sooz. Where's your sense of humor?

You look like you're a million miles away. Susan, are you there? Susan? Susan?"

The faraway look remained in Susan's eyes. And when she finally spoke, her voice was a hoarse whisper. "Chris, I just had the craziest, most fantastic, most *outrageous* idea of my entire life!"

"Goodness! And to think my dumb imitation inspired it! As a matter of fact, I'm not even sure who—or what—I was imitating! I was just being silly!"

"You were imitating a man." Susan's voice was still that same peculiar whisper. "A boy. You were pretending you were a boy."

"Well, yes, I guess so. But I still don't see . . ."

Suddenly, Chris stopped. A chill had just run down her spine as she realized what her twin was getting at.

"No. You're not serious. Susan Pratt, you couldn't be thinking what I think you're thinking. You couldn't be suggesting . . ."

"It's the perfect plan, Chris!" Susan grabbed her sister's arm. "Don't you see? The best way to find out why boys are the way they are is to pretend to *be* one!"

"But Sooz! It's not that simple!"

Susan, however, was not about to listen to any arguments. "You were just saying yourself, not two minutes ago, that what we girls need is for someone to 'infiltrate behind enemy lines,' right? Well, I didn't agree with the words you used then—and I don't agree now—but the point is the same. Chris, it's the only way! And it's so incredible that no one would *ever* suspect what we were doing!"

"Susan Pratt, I know you're my sister, but I must say that I think that this time, you've gone totally off your rocker!" Chris stood up and, with exaggerated movements, began clearing the table. "I mean, I've heard some crazy ideas in my life, but this one *really* takes the cake! You're not really serious, of course. You didn't believe, even for a second, that I'd ever actually agree to go along with something like that, did you?" She stopped fussing with the dishes and turned to face her twin. "*Did* you?"

She could tell from the look on Susan's face that that was *exactly* what she'd believed.

"I've never known you to back away from a challenge before, Chris."

"Sooz, that's not fair!"

"Especially one that would be so helpful. Not only to you, but also to Holly and Beth . . . and me, of course." She was thinking of Michael Anderson, her latest crush. "Not to mention every other girl you know. Why, every other girl in America could benefit! Every girl in the *world!* You could write magazine articles, go on television. . . . Just think, Chris. You'd be the only teenage girl on the entire planet who knew—and I mean *really* knew—what it was like to be a teenage boy!"

Chris was weakening; Susan could see it. She could feel a sense of triumph rising up from deep inside of her.

Even more than that, she experienced the jubilation that came from embarking upon another Pratt twins' hijinks.

"Wait a second—let me get this straight." Chris sat down at the table once again. "You think one of us should pretend to be a boy. . . ."

"Not 'one of us,' *You.* I think you'd be the best person to do it."

18

"Me? Why?"

"Because you're braver than I am. A better actor, too."

"I'm not so sure about that." Chris couldn't help feeling that her twin was buttering her up. At the same time, however, she was flattered. "Well . . . anyway, you want one of us—me—to pretend to be some made-up boy. . . ."

"Let's say a distant relative. A . . . a cousin. Yes, that's it. One of our cousin's, who lives in some town that's far away."

"Okay. So one of us would pretend to be this . . . this boy cousin for a few days. . . ."

"Oh, more than that." Susan sounded very matter-of-fact. "A week, let's say. Yes, that would probably do it. I know: how about starting this Monday, and ending next Saturday? That way, you wouldn't miss out on cheerleading at the Homecoming Game. And you could go to the Homecoming Dance that night as yourself."

Chris nodded. "Yes, that sounds reasonable." Suddenly she almost jumped out of her chair. "Hey, wait a minute! Here I am, sounding as if I'm agreeing to go along with this far-out scheme. . . ."

"But of course you'll go along with it." Susan sounded so certain about the whole thing.

Chris blinked. "I will?"

"Of course you will. And do you know why?"

"No. Why?"

"First of all, because it's a brilliant scheme. Second, because it's the biggest challenge so far to your career as a prankster. Not to mention your career as . . . how did you put it before? Oh, yes: 'a master of disguise.' And third, because the information you

19

get about boys will be so valuable that you'll be providing a great service to females everywhere."

"I'm still not sure, Sooz."

"Wait a minute. That's because I haven't told you the fourth reason yet."

"Oh, really? And what's that?" Chris doubted that any one argument could possibly be strong enough to change her mind.

Susan, on the other hand, seemed completely confident.

"Because if you agree with my plan and pretend to be a boy for the next week, you'll be able to find out what Scott Stevens *really* thinks about you."

Chris's mouth dropped open. "I hadn't thought of that."

Susan looked positively smug. "Now, I've already got the perfect name for this caper. Remember what Holly said last night, about boys being like marshmallows?"

"Yes . . ."

"And you're going to be masquerading as a boy, right? Let's say our cousin Charlie."

"That is, if I agree to go along with this." Chris stopped all of a sudden. "Hey, wait a minute! We don't have a cousin Charlie!"

"We do now! That is, if you agree." Susan looked at her twin hopefully. "Do you agree, Chris? Are you willing to go along with this brilliant scheme of mine?"

Chris thought for only a second. And then she broke out into a huge grin. "Okay, Sooz. You managed to convince me, after all. I may end up regretting this, but you're right. I can't resist!"

"Fantastic! Well, then, we're about to set the world

on its ear with the greatest practical joke that anyone has ever played in the entire history of the world." Susan's cheeks were pink, and her eyes were bright. "Christine Pratt, you and I are about to embark on the Marshmallow Masquerade!"

Three

Since neither of the twins was the type to waste any time, Susan and Chris immediately set about their new, intriguing task: transforming Chris into someone else. And they had to do it so well that they would convince the world—or at least the students of Whittington High—that Chris was really the twins' cousin.

Charlie Pratt.

A *boy*.

Their first stop was the local shopping mall. After all, Susan reasoned, the very first stop in masquerading as a boy was *looking* like one.

As much as they would have loved to browse in all their favorite shops, Chris and Susan bypassed all the boutiques that specialized in women's clothes. Instead, they headed for a store that neither of them had ever been in before. With a name like The Men's Den, they couldn't help but think they had come to the right place.

As soon as they ventured inside, the salesman who was straightening out a display of neckties near the store's entrance noticed them. He hurried toward them. "Can I . . . *help* you girls?"

"Sure," Chris said cheerfully. "I'm looking for—"

"No, thank you," Susan interrupted her. "We're just browsing. We're looking for, uh, a present for our cousin. Our *boy* cousin."

Satisfied with that explanation, the salesman moved on to a young man who was half-heartedly looking through a display of white shirts.

"Chris, what do you think you're doing?"

"Well, I just thought I'd explain that—"

"Explain what? That you're looking for the kind of outfit a boy might wear because you plan to spend the next week pretending to *be* one?"

"You've got a point there," Chris agreed lamely. "It does sound a bit incredible, doesn't it?"

"Just the *teensiest* bit!"

The girls did a quick survey of The Men's Den's merchandise. Susan noticed some plaid flannel shirts folded on a table, and she headed over that way.

Her twin, however, took quite a different tack.

"Hey, look at these, Sooz! They're kind of pretty!" Chris had zeroed in on a sale rack full of sweaters. They were all half-price . . . and they were all pale colors: blue, beige, and two or three in pink. "I like these pink ones. I wonder what size I am in boys' clothes. . . ."

"Christine Pratt! Put that sweater down immediately!" Susan demanded.

"But why?"

"Because it's pink!"

"But I *like* pink!" Chris blinked. She was surprised

23

by her twin's reaction. After all, she had simply picked out the sweater that she liked the best. It was even on sale.

Susan's next statement, however, put things back in perspective.

"Pink is not for boys. It's a *female* color. Why, I'll bet that's why that sweater's on sale in the first place. You know, 'pink is for girls; blue is for boys.' It starts out from the day a baby is born!"

Chris held on to the sweater possessively. "But why?"

The two girls just stared at each other.

"I don't really know, Chris," Susan finally admitted.

"I mean, it doesn't make any sense. You're right, of course. Pink *is* a color that people associate with girls. But why is it that only girl babies wear it? Is there something wrong with boys wearing pink? Why on earth should it make any difference?"

"And come to think of it," Susan said thoughtfully, "it's perfectly acceptable for girls to wear blue. But if a baby boy were ever dressed in pink, people would be flabbergasted!"

Chris frowned. "I'm beginning to realize that the Marshmallow Masquerade is going to be even harder than I thought. I never really thought about it before, but there are a lot of 'differences' between boys and girls that are totally made-up. Like this business about the color pink. It makes absolutely no sense at all . . . yet everybody just accepts it as *law*!"

"I know. It *is* silly, isn't it? But I'm afraid that as long as you're trying to convince the world that you're really Charlie Pratt, we'd better stick to those dumb rules, whether we like them or not."

24

With a shrug, Chris put the pink sweater back on the rack. "Well, okay. But for the rest of my life, every time I put on something pink, I'm going to be reminded of the fact that it's okay for girls to wear clothes that people associate with boys—things like sneakers and plaid flannel shirts and jeans and even the color blue—but if boys ever try wearing 'girl' things, people laugh at them! Everyone accepts the fact that girls are allowed to try being more like boys, but there's something funny about the idea of boys trying to be more like girls!"

After browsing around the store for a few more minutes, the girls picked out some clothes that looked as if they'd fit Chris while still being loose enough to hide her curves. Everything they chose was dark, boxy, and basically nondescript.

"Do you know what I'm starting to realize, Sooz?" Chris mused once they'd decided on their purchases.

"No, what?"

"Boys' clothes are *boring*! Everything comes in either brown, gray, or blue; all the shirts are cut exactly the same. . . . Why, they hardly get any chance at all to express their individuality through the clothes they wear! Not to mention the fact that they're not supposed to wear clothes like pink or yellow or lavender. . . ."

"Or even fabrics with flowers or polka dots or even *checks* on them!" Susan added.

"Well, there is *one* good thing about boys' clothes," Chris commented a few minutes later as the twins left The Men's Den, armed with several packages.

Susan turned to look at her sister. "What's that?"

"They're all so comfortable! No high-heeled shoes

25

that make it impossible to walk. No tight jeans or skirts with tight waistbands that are supposed to make you look slimmer but make it hard to breathe. No itchy lace around the collar or pantyhose that are always slipping down. . . .

"And no make-up to worry about, either." Chris continued. "Imagine going through an entire date without having to worry about whether your mascara has made it look like you've got two black eyes! Or whether you've rubbed off your eyeshadow so that you've got one eyelid that's blue and one that's not!"

"You know, you're right!" Susan laughed. "When you think about it, the things that girls have to do to be considered 'dressed up' or 'nice-looking' are a lot different from what boys do to get the same effect."

"Next time I go to a fancy party," Chris teased, "I think I'll wear a man's suit. Forget the shoes that hurt and the short skirts you're constantly pulling down over your knees!"

"The only thing I wouldn't want to wear is a necktie." Susan wrinkled her nose. "Not only do they look horribly uncomfortable; they serve absolutely no function at all!"

Suddenly, she grew serious. "You know, Sooz, this Marshmallow Masquerade of ours is turning out to be more educational than I ever dreamed possible. And I haven't even started pretending to be Charlie yet!"

Susan nodded in agreement. The two girls paused to think for a moment, and they found themselves in front of one of the mall's snack bars.

"What do you say we stop off for an ice cream cone?" Susan suggested. "We can take a break before we get down to the business of your hair."

"My hair?" Suddenly realizing what her twin was

referring to, Chris placed a protective hand on her thick, shiny locks. "Oh, no! You're not *serious,* are you? You don't really expect me to cut off all my *hair,* do you?"

Susan bit her lip. "Unless you can come up with some other idea—"

"Anything! I'll do anything! But not that!"

"Well, let's see. You could tuck it under a hat, I suppose. A baseball cap, maybe."

Chris shook her head. "Too risky. If the cap ever fell off, the whole Marshmallow Masquerade would be spoiled. Besides, then I'd have to spend every single minute worrying that even one little strand of hair would manage to work its way out."

"How about a hood, then? You could wear one of those nylon jackets. . . ."

"All the time? Then I'd never be able to go inside. I'd have to stay *outside* all the time." Chris shivered at the mere thought. "No, that'd never work. Not in the middle of November, anyway." She looked at her sister morosely. "I'm afraid you're right, Sooz. If I really want this to work, I'm going to have to go ahead and do it right."

"Gee, Chris. Are you sure? It's not too late to turn back, you know."

Chris stared at her reflection in the window of the snack bar. What she saw was a pretty seventeen-year-old girl . . . with a headful of beautiful hair. She sighed loudly, then said, "I just hope Scott Stevens likes girls with short hair. We'd better forget about our ice cream cones for now. Take me to the nearest barber shop before I change my mind!"

Convincing the barber at the mall's barber shop that

she really did want her hair cut to look like a boy's was no easy feat.

Matter-of-factly, Chris said, "But it's the newest style! You mean you've never heard of 'the boy cut'? Why, it's being featured in all the latest fashion magazines!"

Finally, the barber relented. Within minutes, Chris's locks were strewn all over the floor of Benny's Barber Shop. And the hair that was left lay flat on either side of her head, parted on the side . . . exactly the way a boy would wear it.

"What have I done?" Chris cried, her eyes brimming with tears as she stared at the person in the mirror—a person who, she had to admit, did look very much like a boy.

"Just think," her sister said consolingly, "within a couple of weeks it'll be a lot longer. You know how quickly your hair grows. And in the meantime, you can wear combs and barrettes or even curl it. And before you know it, it'll be as long as mine again. Chris . . . Chris . . . are you still speaking to me?"

Chris looked over at her sister and nodded. "It's for a good cause, right? I'll just keep telling myself that, over and over. It's for a good cause, it's for a good cause. . . ."

Susan felt as if her heart was going to break. "Could you at least *smile*, then? Please?"

Her twin obliged. "You're right. I should stop being such a poor sport. I agreed to do this, and I'm going to do it right. Besides, it's going to be lots of fun, once I start pretending to be Charlie Pratt."

"That's the spirit! I knew I could count on you. Now, I've got one more idea. . . ."

"Uh-oh." Chris's smile faded. "What now? Do I have to join the army? Or get a job with a construction crew? Or . . . ?"

"No, nothing like that!" Susan laughed. "If that's what you're thinking, then you're going to be very relieved when you hear my idea. I was thinking that you should get a pair of glasses."

"Glasses?"

"Right. Eyeglasses. To make you look a little different, that's all. Less like the Christine Pratt that everyone at Whittington High already knows."

"Sooz, that's a great idea! Besides, wearing glasses will make the whole masquerade seem a little bit easier."

"It will? Why?"

"Because," Chris explained, looking a bit rueful, "a pair of eyeglasses will give me something to *hide* behind!"

That night, after dinner, Chris and Susan holed up in Chris's room, armed with all their new purchases.

It was time to put the finishing touches on their new creation, Charlie Pratt.

"Boy, I thought Mom and Dad were going to turn *purple* when they saw my hair!" Chris groaned. She reached up to touch her head, as if she still couldn't quite believe that she had actually gone ahead and had all her hair cut off.

"I wonder if they suspect that we're up to something," Susan mused. "I mean, they both pretended to believe you when you said that you just wanted to try something different, but that may just be because they're not the type to pry."

Chris laughed. "Maybe they're just afraid of what

they might find out if they start asking too many questions! After all, they know all about the kinds of pranks we like to play!"

"Actually," Susan said seriously, "I think they simply *trust* us. They know we have good judgment and that we're not about to do anything to hurt anybody else. Or ourselves, either."

Chris sighed loudly. "I just hope they're right."

Susan detected some reluctance on her twin's part, so she immediately set about rousing her enthusiasm for the Marshmallow Masquerade once again.

"Okay, Chris. Why don't you put on your new clothes so we can see what Charlie Pratt looks like?"

Chris donned the brown pants and the brown plaid flannel shirt that the girls had bought that day. She also put on her running shoes, sold as being suitable for both boys and girls, and took off all her jewelry. Then she stood in front of the full-length mirror that lined the back of her bedroom door.

"I don't know. . . ." She put her hands on her hips and frowned as she examined the image before her. "I guess I look *kind* of like a boy. . . ."

"Here, try the glasses." Susan handed her the round glasses with the tortoiseshell frames that they'd gotten at the mall that afternoon. They were sunglasses, but they were so faintly tinted that they looked very much like prescription eyeglasses.

"Well, they help a little." Chris still sounded doubtful.

"Let's look at it this way," said Susan. "Since we'll be introducing you to people as our cousin Charlie, there's no reason for them to start trying to prove that you're a girl and not a boy, right?"

"That's true. And besides, I'll just have to try really

30

hard to *act* like a boy." Chris thought for a few seconds, and then a worried look crossed her face. "Sooz, what exactly do boys *act* like?"

"Actually, I've been giving a lot of thought to that very question. And I decided that there are two kinds of things that make a boy . . . well, seem like a boy. One kind is biological. You know: deeper voice, broader shoulders, hairier faces. . . ."

"I'll do my best," Chris said warily. She lowered her voice experimentally. "Hi. I'm Charlie Pratt. Glad to meet you." Then, in her own voice, she said, "There. How did that sound?"

"It sounded just fine." Susan smiled encouragingly. "But what I think is even more important is the second category of things that make a boy seem like a boy. And that's the things they say and do. And that, I figure, should be a lot easier for you to imitate."

Chris looked skeptical. "Oh, really? Why?"

"Because those are things that boys have *learned*. And so you can learn them, too. Or at least copy them. It should be especially easy because you'll probably be aware of every single movement you make and every word you say."

"Oh, I know what you mean! You mean like the fact that boys never use words like 'teensy' or 'icky' or even 'cute.' Or that they'll never admit they're nervous before taking a test or giving an oral report in class." Chris was growing excited. "Or that they talk about sports all the time. . . ."

"Exactly. There's nothing biological about those things. That's all behavior that boys have learned to do in order to fit in with all the other boys they know."

Chris grinned ruefully. "Well, then, I guess this is my chance to put to work all the observations I've been making about boys my whole life. It looks like I'll be finding out once and for all if I really *am* such an expert on the opposite sex!"

For the rest of the evening, Chris practiced acting like a boy as Susan coached her carefully. She would have to walk differently and sit differently. She would even have to carry her schoolbooks differently. Instead of holding them against her chest as she walked, the way she usually did, she would have to remember to carry them at her side.

There were a million details to remember—or so it seemed. Buying two cartons of milk at lunch, instead of just one. Gulping that milk out of the carton instead of sipping it through a straw. Disposing of trash by tossing it into the wastepaper basket like a basketball, instead of walking over and dropping it in. Crossing her legs at the ankle, instead of at the knee. The list went on forever.

By the end of the evening, however, Chris was confident that she would, indeed, be able to pretend to be the fictitious character Charlie Pratt. And Susan, watching how well she mastered the voice and the actions and expressions of a teenage boy, had no doubt that the masquerade would be successful. The twins were having a lot of fun, preparing for this caper . . . and they were also learning quite a bit as they were forced to think about things they had never taken the time to think about before.

"You know, Sooz," said Chris once she was certain she could carry off this new prank of theirs, "the more time you and I spend deciding what I have to do to become Charlie Pratt instead of me, the more I'm realizing that a *lot* of the so-called 'differences' between boys and girls are simply things that we've *learned*."

"You're right. I've been noticing the exact same thing." Susan smiled. "See, Chris? The Marshmallow Masquerade just might end up proving what I've been saying all along."

"What's that?"

"That boys and girls really *are* basically the same! We just act so different so much of the time because we think we're *supposed* to!"

"Well, I guess we'll find out soon enough." Chris sighed deeply as she looked at her reflection in the mirror one more time. "In less than thirty-six hours, the Pratt twins are going to launch their brand-new creation upon the world.

"Look out, Whittington High. Here comes Charlie Pratt!"

Four

On Monday morning, two very nervous teenagers were making their way down First Street, toward Whittington High. One of them was Susan Pratt, looking pretty much her usual self. The other, however, was someone that no one at Whittington High— or anyone else in the world, for that matter—had ever met before.

"Are you *sure* I look okay?" demanded Christine Pratt—or *Charlie*, as she was now trying so hard to think of herself.

"For the millionth time, you look *great*, Chris. Oh, I'm sorry; I mean *Charlie*. Your hair is perfect; your clothes are fine. The glasses are just the right touch . . . You're even doing a terrific job of walking differently!"

"That's because my knees are shaking so hard! Oh, Sooz, I know this sounded like a wonderful idea all weekend, while we were planning it, but now that we're actually doing it . . ."

34

"It's just stage fright," Susan said calmly. "Don't worry. All the great actors get it."

"Oh, really?" Her twin didn't sound convinced.

"Sure. Once we get going, you'll forget all about being nervous."

"If you say so . . ."

Susan sounded reassuring. "Look, so far everything is going perfectly smoothly, right? Yesterday I called Beth and told her you were sick in bed with the flu and that you'd be in bed all week. Probably up until the Homecoming Game next Saturday. And she believed me one hundred percent. I'm sure she'll start spreading the word. In fact, I sounded so convincing that she might even take up a collection to send you flowers! And she was extra-sympathetic when she heard that our cousin Charlie was coming to visit this week."

"Holly believed our story, too, when I called her. Hey, I sure did a good job of sounding weak over the phone, didn't I?"

"I'm surprised she didn't send for an ambulance! Anyway, the stage is set for the temporary disappearance of Christine Pratt. . . ."

"And the temporary appearance of *Charlie* Pratt."

Chris shoved her hands deep inside the pockets of her navy-blue wool jacket, one of her father's old ones. The girls had discovered it on Sunday afternoon when they had gone rummaging through the old trunks and cardboard boxes packed away in the attic, in search of clothes and anything else that would help them carry out the Marshmallow Masquerade.

"I don't know," she said, shaking her head slowly. "I felt kind of bad this morning, sneaking out of the house without saying anything to Mom and Dad.

Pretending I'd overslept and didn't have time for breakfast."

Susan looked at her sister and blinked. "And how would you have explained Charlie Pratt showing up at Mom and Dad's breakfast table?"

"I know; we had no choice. I just wish we could let them in on it. Besides, I'm starving."

Susan grinned. "Fortunately, I thought of every detail." She reached into her coat pocket and pulled out an orange and a handful of crackers, wrapped in aluminum foil. "See? I snuck these out of the kitchen. You need your strength for this caper!"

"Thanks, Sooz! You *have* thought of everything!" As she munched on a cracker, however, Chris grew pensive once again. "Well, we got out of the house safely this morning . . . but what are we going to tell Mom and Dad *tomorrow* morning? They're going to think I've got African sleeping sickness if I start missing breakfast every day for the next week!"

Suddenly Susan grabbed her sister's arm. "We'll have to worry about that later. In the meantime, get ready to use your deep voice. See that car over there, the one that just slowed down? That's Holly Anderson and her brother, Michael. They're trying to catch our attention!"

"Oh, no! Sooz, I'm so nervous! I don't know if I can really do this . . ."

"Sure you can, Chris! Just remember that you're taking part in one of the greatest adventures *ever* in the entire history of teenage girls. This is it! The Marshmallow Masquerade is about to begin!"

With Susan's dramatic pronouncement, Chris felt all her muscles tingling. Susan was right. Now that they were finally about to get under way, she *was* excited.

And more than ready to be the first teenage girl who ever became a teenage boy.

"Hi, Susan!" called Holly from the car's open window. "Would you and your cousin like a ride to school?"

Chris and Susan exchanged triumphant glances.

"Sure we would. Thanks!" cried Susan.

"Great. Hop in!"

Once Susan and her "cousin" had scrambled onto the backseat, Holly, sitting in the front seat, turned around and said, "Susan, you've met my brother, Mike, haven't you?"

Mike answered the question for her. "Susan and I are old pals!" he joked, grinning through the rearview mirror. "We go back quite a ways, don't we?"

"We sure do!" Laughing, Susan continued with the joke. She could feel herself blushing. She was so pleased that Mike wanted to kid around with her!

Holly, however, was puzzled. "How . . . where . . . ?"

"We were just teasing, my dear little sister." Mike gave her a brotherly pat on the head. Like Holly, he was blond and good-looking, with blue eyes and an easy smile. "Actually, I've only met Susan a few times. When she was over at our house."

"Oh, I see. And this is your cousin, right?"

"Gee, I'm sorry. I almost forgot to introduce you." Susan had been so involved with Mike—and so happy that he did, indeed, remember her—that for a minute she had forgotten all about the stranger sitting beside her. "This is my cousin, uh, Charlie. Charlie Pratt. He lives in, uh, Chicago. His father and our father—I mean, *my* father—are brothers."

"That's right; I'm from Chicago!" Charlie agreed

heartily. "Are you good friends of Chris and Susan's?"

"I'll say," Holly replied. "Chris and Susan and I have known each other since junior high school. By the way, I'm Holly Anderson, and this is my brother, Michael. He's a freshman at the state university, but he's living at home during his first semester."

"Hello, Holly. Hiya, Mike."

So far, so good. Neither of them seemed to notice anything in the least bit peculiar about Susan Pratt's cousin from Chicago.

"So, Charlie Pratt, what brings you to our little town?" Holly asked. She turned all the way around in her seat in order to get a better look at Charlie.

Suddenly, the way she was acting changed.

It was a slight change, so subtle that Chris would probably never even have noticed if she hadn't been the person at whom the change was directed. The way Holly was looking at Charlie was quite different from the way she'd been looking at Susan. Her blue eyes were shining, her head was cocked to one side, and she was twirling a strand of her long blond hair around her fingers.

My goodness! Holly is *flirting*! thought Chris with amusement. Wow! I guess I really *am* convincing as Charlie Pratt!

But then she remembered something. What about Hank? Holly *had* said that he'd been ignoring her lately . . . but the two of them had just started going out together. It seemed only fair that she give him a chance. . . .

Perhaps I'm reading too much into this, Chris thought. Maybe some girls just flirt with *every* boy they meet, just for the fun of it.

Suddenly, Chris froze.

I'm one of those girls! she thought.

It doesn't matter if I actually *like* the boy I'm talking to . . . or if I even *know* him! It's almost a habit! Nothing more than a game, one of those games we were talking about the other night, the type that boys and girls both get caught up in playing all the time.

And it never once occurred to me that I might be pretending to be interested in somebody when I wasn't, that I might be hurting his feelings in the long run by paying special attention to him at first and then ignoring him from then on. . . .

Chris was so absorbed in her observations that she never got around to answering Holly's question. Fortunately, Susan filled in for her.

"Charlie's just visiting our family for the week, until this weekend. In fact, he's going back to Chicago first thing Saturday morning. Right, Charlie?"

"Oh, uh, right, Susan."

"Just this week, huh?" Suddenly, Holly turned away, obviously having lost interest in him because he wasn't going to be around for very long. "Gee, too bad Chris is sick during your visit," she said off handedly.

"Well, I figured I'd sit in on some of her classes," explained Charlie. "Then I can fill her in on the lectures and help her with the homework. That way she won't miss any school, even though she's got such a bad case of the flu. Besides, I'm a senior, too, so it won't hurt me to go to some of my cousin's classes while I'm here."

"Ummm." It was clear that Holly was no longer interested in whatever Charlie Pratt had to say.

Mike, however, was ready to be friendly. "Well,

Charlie, maybe you'd like to get together after school one day this week. You know, shoot some baskets, maybe watch a game on TV. Hey, I've got a whole scrapbook full of clippings about basketball players. I'd be happy to show it to you sometime!"

Chris gulped. "Sure, Mike. Sounds great."

How peculiar it was that simply because Charlie happened to be a boy, Mike just assumed he was interested in sports. And that he enjoyed playing them, too.

Gee, that must put boys under a lot of pressure, she mused. Here Charlie doesn't even *know* Mike, and yet he's supposed to play basketball with him!

Then she realized that *she* was the one who'd be playing basketball with Mike Anderson.

"Of course," she said hastily, "I may be pretty busy all week . . ."

But Chris's lame protest was lost. The car had just pulled up in front of Whittington High.

"Here we are!" Holly cried gaily.

The three of them climbed out of the car, thanking Mike for the ride. His parting words were "See you around, Susan! And Charlie, stop over at my house anytime!"

Once he had driven away, Holly said, "Oh, look, Susan! There's Hank! Gee, I think I'll pretend I didn't see him, and just 'happen' to walk by him. See you two later! Oh, nice meeting you, Charlie!"

Once again, Chris thought about how Holly had been flirting with Charlie in the car just minutes earlier. And now here she was, running off to catch some other boy's attention . . . right in front of him!

Chris shook her head slowly. Gee, if I really were a boy, I bet I'd be pretty confused right now. Holly doesn't seem to realize that Charlie's got feelings, too!

She was about to turn to her twin and say, "Well, Holly would probably be amazed to hear that flirting with every boy she meets isn't necessarily going to help her social life!" But Susan sighed loudly.

"Boy, I can't believe that Holly just left us here like that! All because she wanted to run and catch Hank's attention. As if he were more important than we are! That's pretty rude, don't you think?"

"I can't believe you said that," said Chris. "I was just thinking the same thing . . . but for a different reason!"

"Really? What do you mean?"

"Well, a few minutes ago Holly was flirting with Charlie, and now, right in front of him, she's running off to find some other boy!"

Susan was dumbfounded. "What on earth are you talking about, Chris? *Holly* was flirting with *Charlie*?"

"Well, sure. Don't tell me you didn't notice how differently she reacted to you and to Charlie."

"No . . . I didn't notice anything odd. Why? What happened? Did I miss something?"

Chris opened her mouth to explain—and then promptly shut it again.

"Never mind, Sooz. I'll explain later. In the meantime, let me just say that in the last ten minutes or so, ever since I became Charlie Pratt, I've learned more about being a boy than in the entire seventeen years before that!"

Five

While the first day of the Marshmallow Masquerade had started out smoothly enough, it wasn't long before Chris–as–Charlie Pratt ran into her first major problem.

It started in homeroom, as soon as she wandered into the classroom, trying to look a bit confused. She nodded politely to some of Chris's friends and was relieved to see that they simply looked back at her blankly. So far, her disguise was working!

Once she sat down, however, the trouble began.

"Hey, who's the new kid?" someone behind her demanded in a gruff voice.

Chris turned around and found herself looking up at Eddie McKay, a tough, belligerent senior who had a reputation for being Whittington High's biggest bully. He and Chris traveled in very different circles, and the two of them had never payed very much attention to each other before.

Suddenly, all that changed.

Eddie and his two buddies, Frank Hollinger and Jimmy Nelson, were standing together, looking Charlie Pratt over. And their attitude was anything but friendly.

"Hello!" Chris said in her deepest Charlie voice. "I'm Charlie Pratt. Chris Pratt's cousin . . ."

"Oh, yeah?" Menacingly, Eddie raised his chin into the air. "So what makes you think you're allowed to sit in my seat?"

Chris knew very well that there was no such thing as "Eddie's seat." There was no assigned seating in her homeroom. Students could sit anywhere they pleased, and they tended to take different seats practically every day, depending upon who came in early and who came in late.

However, that was something that Charlie Pratt probably wouldn't know. And even if he did, this wasn't the time and place to start quoting the rules. Not to someone like Eddie McKay.

"Gee, I'm sorry." Charlie jumped up and headed toward a different chair. "I didn't know that was your seat. Believe me, it won't happen again."

"Hey, what a sissy!" cried Frank. "Aren't you even going to fight for you seat?"

"Well . . . no," Charlie said evenly. "If this seat belongs to, uh, your friend over there, he's welcome to have it back. Besides, I don't care where I sit."

"Oh, you don't, huh?" Eddie came over to where Chris was standing and stood very close to her. With a hostile look in his eyes, he peered down at her. "Do you want to know what I think, Charlie Pratt? I think you're a wimp! Yeah, a real wimp! And I'll tell you something else. I don't like wimps! Now, what do you think of that?"

Chris gulped. "I, uh, you . . ."

The three boys were now laughing together. But their laughter was cold and mean. Chris could feel herself turning red.

Fortunately, the bell rang at that moment. All the students in Chris's homeroom, including Eddie and his pals, sat down. For the moment, at least, she was safe.

Whew! That was scary! she thought. Boy, Eddie McKay has never said two words to me before. That is, when I was a girl. But once he thought I was another boy, he felt he had to prove something to me. That he was the toughest or something. I'd better make sure I keep away from him and his friends!

That was not going to be easy, however, Chris discovered quickly.

During homeroom, she didn't have time to worry about Eddie. She was too busy explaining to Ms. White, the homeroom teacher, all about how Charlie was Chris Pratt's cousin, sitting in on her classes while she was out sick.

But once the bell rang, signifying that homeroom was over, Eddie came over to Chris again. Frank and Jimmy were still in tow.

"Listen, you," Eddie hissed, pointing a finger at Chris. "I don't like your face, you hear me? And you'd better keep out of my way . . . or else!"

Before Chris could think of anything to say, he was gone.

What a creep! she thought as she gathered up her schoolbooks, being careful to carry them at her side. I sure hope he doesn't bother me again!

She forgot all about him, however, as she became absorbed, once again, in playing the part of Charlie, someone who didn't know a soul at Whittington High, someone who was completely lost in the maze of corridors and classrooms.

It never even occurred to her that for the next few days, Eddie McKay, a boy she hardly even knew, was going to try his hardest to make her life miserable.

The rest of the morning passed quickly and without mishap. The students in Chris's classes accepted without question the fact that Charlie was Chris's cousin, that he was sitting in on her classes to help her keep from falling behind in her schoolwork while she was sick . . . and that he was a boy. Susan's comment over the weekend—that Chris wouldn't have too hard a time being convincing as Charlie because no one would be out to prove that she *wasn't* a boy—was proving to be one hundred percent correct.

If anything, Chris-as-Charlie was disappointed by how *little* attention she was receiving. Even when she made an effort to talk to other students in her class, they merely answered her politely, then moved on to talk to their friends.

That is, until lunch period, when Chris spotted Scott Stevens, sitting in the school cafeteria, all by himself.

This is my big chance! thought Chris. It's now or never!

Her heart was pounding as she made her way across the cafeteria toward Scott's table, tray in hand. She had remembered to get *two* cartons of milk . . . and no straws. How she would manage to *drink* them both, however, was another matter entirely.

At this point, she reminded herself, drinking all that milk should be the *least* of your concerns!

"Hi! Mind if I sit down?" Chris said in her best

45

Charlie voice. By now, her heart was beating so loudly that she was certain everyone in the room could hear it.

"Nope. Have a seat." Scott glanced at Charlie for only a second before turning back to his tuna fish sandwich.

But Chris was not about to let such a golden opportunity slip by. She sat down right opposite him.

Her initial inclination was to be flirtatious.

Whoa—wait a minute! You're not Chris. . . . You're *Charlie*, remember? You've got to act as if you're just one of the guys. And as if Scott Stevens is also just one of the guys.

As she looked into his green eyes and felt her heart melting, she knew that that was going to be anything but easy.

"My name is Charlie. Charlie Pratt." Fortunately, using a deeper voice than usual helped keep it from shaking. She sounded casual, exactly the way she wanted to sound.

"Hello. I'm Scott Stevens. Are you new here at Whittington High?"

"Well, not exactly. I mean, I'm Chris Pratt's cousin. I'm visiting from Chicago. Do you, uh, *know* Chris?"

"Sure!" Scott brightened at the mention of her name. Or was she just imagining it? "Chris is in my history class sixth period."

"Really? Well, she's out sick. A pretty bad case of the flu. She has to stay in bed for a few days—maybe even all week."

"Gee, that's tough."

"Yeah. So I'm sitting in on her classes for her. You know, so I can fill her in on what she missed, help her with her homework, stuff like that."

"Hey, that's awfully nice of you! Especially since this is kind of a vacation for you, isn't it? I mean, coming here all the way from Chicago to visit Chris's family."

"Well . . . I don't mind."

Chris was beginning to feel brave. The more she talked—and the longer she was able to convince people that she was Charlie Pratt—the easier the Marshmallow Masquerade became. And the temptation to take advantage of such a golden opportunity to find out more about what Scott thought of Chris was irresistible.

"In fact," she went on, "I'm glad I can help old Chris out. After all, she's a great girl." When Scott remained silent, seeming more interested in his tuna fish sandwich than in discussing the girls he knew, Chris-as-Charlie couldn't resist adding, "Don't you think so?"

"Huh?" Scott looked startled. "Oh, sure. I guess so. I mean, I don't really *know* your cousin very well."

Chris was flabbergasted. Here she thought that she and Scott were becoming good friends! She was certainly making an effort. Talking to him every chance she got, plotting ways to run into him between classes and after school . . . even going so far as to offer to help him study for that big exam on the Civil War.

Why, she thought she was being positively *brazen,* making it obvious that she liked Scott Steven very much. And it turned out that he hadn't even noticed!

Disappointed, she turned to her lunch.

"So, Charlie, are you a high school student, too?" Scott asked congenially.

Chris nodded. "I'm a senior. At, uh, Chicago High."

Once she said that, she realized how ridiculous that sounded.

Why, Chicago is a huge city, and it must have dozens of high schools! she thought. There's not just one called "Chicago High," the way there is here in Whittington.

But Scott didn't seem to notice. Once again, Susan's contention—that no one would notice anything peculiar simply because they had no reason to start looking for inconsistencies—was proving to be true.

"Wow. It must be exciting, living in a place like Chicago. What's it like?"

Chris nearly choked on her cheeseburger. She had never been to Chicago. But Scott was looking at her, expecting an answer.

"It's, uh, pretty nice. It's quite a bit . . . *bigger* than Whittington.

"Yeah, I can imagine."

"Have you ever been there?"

"Nope."

Suddenly, Chris relaxed. "Oh, well. You'd really like it. It's got great museums, and . . . and parks and lots of different kinds of restaurants. It's really a fun place to live."

"Gee, it sounds terrific. What about your school? Are you interested in sports?"

Chris hesitated. She was already dreading an afternoon of shooting baskets with Holly's brother. The idea of doing the same thing with the captain of the basketball team was simply too much!

"Well . . . yes. But I don't have much time for

48

sports. I've got a pretty heavy course load this year. How about you?"

"I play basketball. In fact, I'm the captain of Whittington High's team."

"No kidding!" Chris didn't want Scott to lose interest in Charlie, and she knew how important sports were to him, so she added brightly, "I like to watch the games on television, though."

"Hey! Me, too! Do you like basketball?"

"Oh, sure. I like basketball, football, baseball. . . ."

Scott was growing excited. This was clearly a subject that he found extremely interesting. "What's your favorite team?"

Chris's mind went blank. Even though she knew a little bit about sports, all of a sudden she couldn't remember the name of a single team. "I, uh, like the Cubs." It was the first name that came to mind.

"Oh, sure! That's because you're from Chicago! It stands to reason that you'd be loyal to the home team!"

Chris breathed a sigh of relief.

"But I'm not talking about baseball. What about basketball?"

"Oh." This was turning out to be harder than she ever expected! "I like . . . the Chicago team."

"The Bulls, huh? Yeah, they're okay. I like them, too."

Chris desperately hoped that their conversation about sports had come to an end. She was on the verge of trying to change the subject to something less risky when Scott said, "Listen, Charlie, I've got to run. The coach called a special meeting at twelve-thirty, so I'd better get going. But I really enjoyed talking to you.

How'd you like to come over to my house after school one day this week?"

Chris almost gasped.

Stay calm, she reminded herself. You're Charlie, remember?

Sounding so matter-of-fact that even she was impressed, she said, "Sure, Scott. Sounds great!"

"Okay, how about tomorrow?"

"Uh . . . okay. Tomorrow sounds fine."

"We can walk over to my house right after school. After all, you probably don't know your way around Whittington too well, do you?"

"Uh, no, I don't." Chris was still in such shock that it was difficult for her to talk.

"Okay, then, Charlie! Take it easy, and I'll see you tomorrow!"

Chris just nodded. "Taking it easy," she knew, was going to be anything *but* easy!

For the rest of the day, Chris was on cloud nine. Imagine—she was going over to Scott's *house*! Finally, after having a crush on the captain of the basketball team for ages, he had invited her over.

The fact that it was Charlie Pratt he had invited, and not his girl cousin Chris, hardly bothered her at all.

Besides, she reasoned, it's better this way. The more time I spend with Scott, the better I'll get to know him. And the better I know him, the easier it will be for me to find out how he really feels about Christine Pratt.

Chris was in such a good mood, in fact, that when she ran into Eddie McKay and his two buddies as she was strolling out of the school building, she didn't even think about their encounter of earlier that day.

That is, until he said in a wheedling tone, "Well, well, well. If it isn't Charlie Pratt, Chris Pratt's wimpy cousin from Chicago."

Why is Charlie "wimpy" just because he didn't want to get into a fight over a stupid chair? Chris wondered, suddenly angry. I never realized before that boys are constantly expected to act so tough! At least where creeps like Eddie McKay are involved!

But she didn't have much of a chance to think about that injustice. The three boys came toward her, edging her over to the brick wall of the school and surrounding her. For the moment, she was trapped.

"Hey, Charlie," said Eddie, "I think you stole my pen."

"What are you talking about?" Chris was trying to sound tough. Instead, she sounded scared.

"You know exactly what I'm talking about," Eddie returned. "I had my pen when I went into homeroom this morning, and when I got to my first class, I looked in my pocket and it was gone. And I know for a fact that *you're* the one who took it!"

"I did not!"

"Hey," Frank said, taking a step closer to her. "If Eddie says you took his pen, then you took his pen."

"But I swear—"

"You're not calling me a liar, *are* you?" Eddie's dark eyes narrowed. "Well, *are* you?"

Chris had an idea. "Look. I'll *show* you that I don't have your pen." She stuck her hand into her shirt pocket and brought out the pen she had been using all day, one of the inexpensive plastic ones that are sold everywhere. "See? This is my pen. It's the only one I've got."

"That's my pen!" Eddie cried.

Chris was starting to panic. "It's possible that your pen *looks* like this, Eddie. I mean, there are a lot of them around. But there's no way that it's your pen."

Eddie stepped right up to her. Poking her in the chest with his index finger, he said, "You're a thief, and you're a liar. And if you think I'm going to let you get away with that, you're crazy."

"Yeah," said Jimmy. "You're crazy! *Nobody* steals from Eddie and gets away with it!"

"I want to have this out with you, buddy. Man to man. Friday, after school. Right here. We'll settle this once and for all."

"You mean you want to *fight*?" Chris was so frightened that she could hardly talk.

Eddie just laughed cruelly. "And don't get any funny ideas about trying to hide from me. I'll come and find you. Once I've decided that I'm going to show somebody who's boss around here, I don't change my mind."

"Yeah! Eddie doesn't change his mind!" Frank said.

With one final poke of his finger, Eddie said, "See you on Friday, Charlie. After school. Right on this spot. And if you know what's good for you, you'll bring along plenty of Band-Aids!"

Whooping as if Eddie had just said the most clever thing any of them had ever heard in their entire lives, the three boys took off.

Chris just stood there, shaking.

Eddie McKay, the school bully, had just challenged her to a fight! And he'd made it clear that he wasn't about to take "no" for an answer!

It didn't make any sense. And she certainly hadn't done anything to bring it on herself. Why, Charlie

Pratt hadn't done anything to offend *anybody*! Yet here he was, after only one day at Whittington High, expected to have it out with Eddie in just a few days.

There was one way to get around it, or course. Charlie could suddenly leave town, going back to Chicago . . . where he was safe, far away from Eddie McKay and his friends.

The only problem was that then the Marshmallow Masquerade would have to be cut short.

And, as scared as she was, letting a bully like Eddie McKay bring that about wasn't something that Chris was about to let happen.

Not if she could help it.

Six

"Sooz, I've got to talk to you!"

"I'm all ears! I can't wait to hear every single detail of the first day of the Marshmallow Masquerade!"

The twins were at Fozzy's, Whittington's ice cream parlor, where they'd decided to meet after school in order to discuss Charlie Pratt's debut. They were sitting at a round white table that was off to one side and therefore afforded them some privacy. In front of each of them was a huge chocolate ice cream soda.

But while Susan was already wolfing hers down, Chris's just sat there, untouched. As a matter of fact, the scoop of chocolate ice cream on top of the frosty glass was starting to melt.

After a few seconds, Susan realized that her sister was silent. When she looked up from her soda, having just consumed almost half of it, she saw that Chris was merely staring at hers. And the expression on her face was one of total dispair.

"Chris! What's wrong? Oh, no, don't tell me someone saw through the masquerade already!"

Chris shook her head slowly. "No, it's nothing like that."

"Well, that's a relief!"

"It's something *worse* than that. Much worse!"

"Uh-oh." Susan couldn't imagine what could possibly be so terrible. But *something* was up. Why, Chris looked as if she was on the verge of crying.

"Do you know who Eddie McKay is?"

Susan immediately made a face. "Oh, yuck. He's that bully who's always acting tough. Getting into trouble. And picking fights."

"That's the one." Chris sighed loudly. "Guess who his latest target is."

"Oh, no! Not Charlie Pratt!"

"None other. Oh, Sooz, he's challenged me—I mean Charlie—to a fight! This Friday, right after school!"

Chris proceeded to fill her twin in on the details of both the encounters she'd had that day with Eddie McKay and his friends, Jimmy and Frank, even quoting Eddie's warning about what would happen if Charlie tried to hide from him. "I'll come and find you," he had said. "Once I've decided that I'm going to show somebody who's boss around here, I don't change my mind." She ended by saying that she suspected Eddie was going to go out of his way for the rest of the week to scare her every chance he got.

Susan just listened, spellbound. By that point, her chocolate ice cream was also beginning to melt.

"Chris, that's terrible! What are you going to do? Do you have any ideas?"

"Do *I* have any ideas! Susan Pratt, you're the

mastermind behind the Marshmallow Masquerade! *You* got me into this; *you* should get me out of it!"

Susan thought for a few seconds. "Don't panic, Chris. After all, we have until Friday afternoon. It's only Monday. We have lots of time before then to come up with something." She hesitated. "Of course, we could always just call off the Marshmallow Masquerade. Make up some story about Charlie having to go back to Chicago and Chris having a sudden, miraculous recovery from the flu."

"I already thought of that," Chris said morosely. "But I don't want to end the Marshmallow Masquerade now! I still think it's a great idea. And it's obviously working. I mean, I certainly managed to convince Eddie and his pals that I was a boy, right?"

Susan laughed half-heartedly. "That's true. Even so, Chris, this could be dangerous. That Eddie's an awful creep. . . ."

"But that's the point!" Chris cried. "Eddie *is* a creep! And I'll be darned if I'm going to let him spoil a good thing! Here the Marshmallow Masquerade is in full swing. I cut my hair, bought all these clothes. . . . And I've already managed to convince half of Whittington High that I really am Charlie Pratt! Even Scott Stevens . . ."

"Oh, Chris!" squealed Susan. "Do you mean you talked to Scott today? How did it go? What did he say?"

All of a sudden, Chris smiled triumphantly. "He invited Charlie over to his house, tomorrow after school!"

"Wow! You sure are a fast worker!" Susan grinned teasingly. "Did you manage to find out anything about how Scott feels about Charlie's cousin?"

"Well, no. Not really." Chris turned back to her chocolate soda thoughtfully. Just because the ice cream was a little bit melted, she decided, there was no reason to let it go to waste. Within a few seconds she had downed a good portion of it. "Although I did learn *one* thing that was kind of interesting."

"Really? What?" Susan leaned forward, anxious to hear about her twin's latest discovery.

"Here I thought I was making a big play for Scott. You know, letting him know, in all these really obvious ways, that I thought he was special. And it turns out that he didn't even *notice*! I guess he just thought I was being friendly or something!"

Susan nodded earnestly. "That supports my theory that the world would be a much better place if boys and girls could just be *direct* with each other."

"Oh, Susan!" Chris cried, exasperated. "What do you expect me to do? Go up to him and say, 'Scott, do you know what chapters we're supposed to read for history tonight? Oh, and by the way, did you know I've developed such an incredible crush on you that I've actually started going to basketball games, even though I think watching basketball is about as much fun as watching grass grow?' Come on, Sooz! Give me a break!"

"Actually," her sister replied with annoying calmness, "I was thinking how much easier all this would have been if you had just called him up on the phone and asked him out."

Chris's mouth dropped open.

"Well, why on earth not? If he'd been the one to get a crush on you first, that's exactly what *he* would have done, right?"

"Yes, but—"

"I don't think that boys are any better at dialing telephones than girls are, are they? Especially since Touch-Tone phones have made the whole process so simple!"

Chris burst out laughing. "I can't argue with you on that, Sooz. You're absolutely right. We're all still following rules that must be a million years old!"

"There were no telephones a million years ago."

"Well, then, I guess it was cave*men* who used to ask cave*women* out all the time! Anyway, I agree with you that the whole thing is pretty silly, especially in this day and age." Chris sighed deeply, toying with her straw. "Unfortunately, I'm not sure that I'm brave enough to be such a maverick."

"You're brave enough to cut your hair and pretend to be a boy!" Susan protested.

"That's different! That's . . . well, a prank. Calling up Scott and asking him out would be for *real*. Besides, when's the last time *you* called a boy?"

Susan blushed. Chris was right, of course. It was easy to urge someone else to do something a bit out of the ordinary. Doing it herself, however, was another matter entirely.

Even so, she didn't want to lose face with her twin.

"Well, I haven't tried it . . . yet. But maybe I will, one of these days."

Chris's dark brown eyes lit up. "Oh, really? And who, may I ask, will be the lucky recipient of your telephone call?"

By now, Susan was beet red. "That, my dear twin," she said, keeping her eyes glued to what was left of her ice cream soda, "is for me to know and you to find out!"

It was time to change the subject, Susan decided.

"But I don't want to talk about my social life; I want to hear all about what happened today. Tell me everything, right from the start. And don't you *dare* leave out one single detail!"

"Okay. But before I start, let me ask you one thing." Chris was grinning mischievously.

"What?"

"If boys can drink two cartons of milk at lunch . . ."

"Yes?"

"Is it okay for them to have *two* ice cream sodas after school?"

Susan pretended to ponder that question with great seriousness. "Well, I guess so. On one condition, of course."

"What's that?"

"That the girl that they're with gets to help drink it!"

Chris immediately flagged down their waitress. "Excuse me. I'd like another chocolate ice cream soda, please!"

The waitress looked over at Chris-as-Charlie and shook her head slowly. "You boys never cease to amaze me!" she said cheerfully. "First of all, you can consume more food at one sitting than an entire roomful of girls. And second, you never put on an ounce!" She shrugged, then said, "One more chocolate ice cream soda, coming up!"

Chris and Susan just looked at each other and laughed.

"My goodness!" exclaimed Mrs. Pratt as she sat at the dinner table, eyeing her daughters' plates. "You two don't seem very hungry tonight!"

"Maybe Susan and Chris are simply getting ready for Thanksgiving," Mr. Pratt commented, heaping a second helping of mashed potatoes onto his plate. "After all, Turkey Day is only a week and a half away. I'd say they're pretty clever, starting to save up room so far in advance!"

Instead of laughing at their father's bad jokes, the way they usually did, the twins merely exchanged wary glances.

"Let's just say that we've both got kind of a stomach ache," Chris said. She glanced down at the small serving of salad she'd put on her plate, wondering how she would ever manage to eat it.

"That's right," Susan agreed. She forced herself to bite into a biscuit. "We're, um, kind of full because we stopped off after school for a little snack."

"Uh-oh," Mr. Pratt teased. "Don't tell me you girls have been eating up all of Fozzy's ice cream inventory again! Having another one of your celebrations, no doubt!"

"Daddy, how did you know we went to Fozzy's?" Chris cried.

Susan, however, was even more alert. "Wait a minute. What do you mean, 'having another one of our celebrations'?"

Mr. and Mrs. Pratt looked at each other. For a second, they both looked terribly guilty. But then they burst out laughing.

"Don't tell me you know!" Chris squealed. "How on earth did you ever find out about the Marshmallow Masquerade?"

"The *what?*" Mr. and Mrs. Pratt demanded in unison.

The twins started to laugh, too.

"Don't you think that your own parents *know* you two by now?" said Mrs. Pratt. "We may not know all the details—or your secret code words, either—but we can certainly figure out when you girls are up to something!"

"All that whispering and giggling behind closed doors," Mr. Pratt said. "Rummaging through my old clothes in the attic, sneaking out of the house without any breakfast . . . And then there's that outlandish haircut that Chris got on Saturday!"

"Now that all this is out in the open," Mrs. Pratt said, "how about you girls telling us all about this . . . What did you call it? 'Marshmallow Masquerade'?"

It was a relief for Chris and Susan to tell their parents all about their scheme—including how well it was going so far. Not wanting them to worry, however, Chris left out the part about Eddie McKay and his threats. Susan, following her lead, remained silent as well. The girls shared the same philosophy where their shenanigans were concerned: If they got themselves *into* scrapes, then it was their responsibility to get themselves *out* of them, as well.

When they had finished explaining the Marshmallow Masquerade—how it had come to be and how it was progressing—the twins sat back and waited to see their parents' reactions. It occurred to them that their parents might insist that they abandon it entirely . . . but somehow they suspected that their mother and father would support them in what they were doing.

"Well," said Mrs. Pratt, her eyes twinkling, "if I remember correctly, when I was a teenage girl, I was pretty baffled by teenage boys myself. I would have loved the chance to find out more about those puzzling creatures."

"'Creatures'!" exclaimed Mr. Pratt. "I was never a 'creature'! At least I don't think I was. And I don't think I am one now. . . . Am I?"

"You're one of the lucky ones, dear," Mrs. Pratt replied with a perfectly straight face. "*You* managed to outgrow it!"

"So you don't mind?" asked Chris hopefully. "I mean, now that you know all about it, you think it's okay if we continue?"

"Well, you're not missing any school because of it," Mrs. Pratt observed. "You're not hurting anyone, either. And I suppose it *is* educational."

"Besides," said Mr. Pratt, "you might as well get some more mileage out of that haircut of yours!"

"Yippeee!" cried Susan. "The Marshmallow Masquerade goes on!"

"And do you know what the best part about having Mom and Dad know all about it is?" Chris asked in a teasing tone.

"No, what?"

"Now I don't have to miss breakfast anymore!"

Happily, she stuck a big forkful of salad into her mouth.

Seven

As she dressed for school on Tuesday morning, Chris was enthusiastic about embarking upon day two of the Marshmallow Masquerade. Her success of the day before, her parents' support, and the prospect of going over to Scott Stevens's house after school had all put her in a good mood. Even her fears about Eddie McKay were stashed away at the back of her mind, at least for the moment. As a matter of fact, she was actually whistling as she left the house, disguised as Charlie Pratt.

Her twin picked up on her good mood immediately.

"So, Chris, I see you're all ready for another day as Charlie Pratt, Whittington High's number-one mystery man," she teased.

"That's right. I'm really looking forward to it. In fact, maybe you and I should *run* to school this morning, so we can get there all the sooner!"

"Gee," Susan said wistfully, "I was kind of hoping that Mike Anderson would give us a ride again." And then, as if she'd just realized what she'd said, she added, "I mean, I really like Holly, and, uh, it'd be fun to see her again. I see so little of her these days."

"You've got to be kidding, Sooz! Holly's over our house so often that Mom and Dad probably think they've got triplets, instead of twins!"

As she was puzzling over her twin's remark, however, Chris suddenly realized what it all meant.

Of *course*! she thought. Mike Anderson! Only yesterday Susan was saying that there was a boy she was thinking of calling. And I had no idea who she meant. But it's got to be Mike!

For a moment, she was tempted to tease Susan about it. But Chris knew her twin sister very well. She was a person who valued her privacy. When there was something she decided to keep a secret, she really meant it. She wasn't at all like Chris, who went around telling everyone *everything* about herself!

No, Chris decided, she wouldn't say anything to Susan.

What she *would* do, however, was try to play matchmaker. Not her, exactly, but Charlie Pratt.

It's the least that Charlie can do for Susan, she thought with satisfaction. After all, Susan is the one who thought up the Marshmallow Masquerade—who *created* Charlie Pratt—in the first place!

Once Whittington High came into view, however, Chris forgot all about matching up her sister with Mike Anderson.

She suddenly realized what the fact that it was Tuesday meant.

On Tuesdays, Chris Pratt had gym class.

"Oh, no!" she cried, stopping in her tracks. "Sooz, I just remembered something!"

"What?"

"I have *gym* today! What am I going to do? I mean, what is Charlie going to do?"

Instead of offering her sympathy, however, Susan grew excited.

"Chris, that's fantastic! This could well be one of the shining moments of the Marshmallow Masquerade!"

"What are you *talking* about?" Chris wailed. "Surely you don't expect Charlie—I mean *me*—to take part in a boys' gym class!"

"Why not? Just think, Chris, you'd get to hear what the boys talk about in the locker room! Well, maybe not . . . but at least you'd get a glimpse of what boys are like when they're alone. How they treat each other, what they talk about . . . That's exactly what we were talking about with Holly and Beth last Friday night, remember? Being a 'fly on the wall' and all that?

"It's simple, too. Just go up to Mr. Nagle, the boys' gym teacher, and explain that you're visiting the school from Chicago and that you're Chris Pratt's cousin and all that, and that you'd like to take gym so you can get some exercise. . . ."

"Wait a minute! What will I wear? And where will I change? And . . . and . . ."

Susan remained undaunted. "Those are all just minor details. I have great faith in you, Chris. You'll come up with a way to get around the tricky parts. After all, this is *such* an opportunity! Oooh, I'm so thrilled!"

By the time Susan and her twin sister parted, Chris had actually agreed to go along with it.

But as she walked into her homeroom, her heart sank.

Oh, no! she thought. Scott Stevens *also* has gym second period! He'll be in that gym class with me!

Even Eddie McKay's mean looks, all through homeroom, didn't bother her. For a moment, she had something a lot scarier than a bully's threats to worry about!

For the rest of the morning, Chris tried hard to see the positive side of what she was about to do during third period. Maybe Susan was right. Perhaps this really was her "golden opportunity." After all, gym class was the only time during the school day that the boys were separated completely from the girls. All male students, a male gym teacher . . . and absolutely, positively no girls.

For the first time, Chris was going to experience being "one of the boys."

When third period rolled around and Chris-as-Charlie was striding into the boys' gym in search of Mr. Nagle, she was still nervous. But she was also excited. After all, she was about to enter territory that no girl had ever entered before. And that, in itself, was no small achievement!

"Are you Mr. Nagle?" Chris asked, knowing full well that the muscular man in the gray Whittington High T-shirt with a whistle hanging around his neck was, indeed, the boys' gym teacher.

"Yes, I am," he replied. "What can I do for you, son?"

Chris felt a small surge of triumph, just as she did when anyone she talked to assumed that the short-haired person in the baggy shirt and sneakers was a boy. "I'm Charlie Pratt. My cousins Chris and Susan are students here at Whittington High. . . ."

"Ah, yes. I know Chris. She's a cheerleader, isn't she? And she's on the girls' swim team, too, I believe."

"That's right." The fact that Mr. Nagle knew Chris—as Chris, of course—made the triumph of fooling him even sweeter. "Anyway, I'm from Chicago, but I'm visiting my cousins this week. Chris is out sick, though, and I've been going to her classes for her, to help her keep from falling behind. She has gym scheduled for this period, and of course I can't take gym with the girls. . . ."

Mr. Nagle laughed heartily. "No, of course not, Charlie. That wouldn't work out too well, now, would it?"

If you only knew, thought Chris, smiling to herself. "I guess not. Anyway, I was wondering if I could participate in the *boys*' gym class, just for this week."

"Sure, Charlie," he replied. "Why not?"

Chris had a very good answer to that question, too. But it was one that, for now, she would have to keep to herself.

"I see you've already got sneakers, Charlie. I'm pretty sure I've got an extra set of gym shorts and a T-shirt around that you can wear—"

"Oh, that's okay, Mr. Nagle," Chris sputtered. "I mean, uh, I don't mind wearing these clothes."

Mr. Nagle glanced at Charlie Pratt quizzically. "You'll be working up quite a sweat in my class. I think you'd be much more comfortable in a pair of gym shorts. Besides, it's a school rule."

Chris's heart sank.

But before she could say, "Susan Pratt, what have

you gotten me into *now*?" Mr. Nagle had stepped into the small office near the entrance to the gym, picked up some neatly folded clothes from a shelf, and returned to hand them to her.

"I'm afraid all we've got left is extra-large," he said apologetically. "And there are no more T-shirts, so you'll have to wear this sweatshirt."

"Thanks, Mr. Nagle." Well, thought Chris, at least if they're baggy, they'll help hide the fact that Charlie Pratt is shaped more like a seventeen-year-old girl than a seventeen-year-old boy!

"I'll have somebody show you where the lockers are." Mr. Nagle glanced up at the stream of boys who had started filing into the gym. "Blake!" he called. "Come on over here for a minute!"

Peter Blake, the "school nerd" that Chris and Holly had been joking about just a few nights earlier, sauntered over wearing a friendly grin. As always, his dark hair was just a bit too long, and a few strands in front kept falling into his eyes.

"Pratt, this is Blake. Blake, would you please show Pratt here where the empty lockers are? He'll be taking gym with us this week."

"Sure, Mr. Nagle," Peter Blake agreed cheerfully. "Come with me. I'll get you set up."

"By the way, my first name is Charlie," said Chris as they walked across the gym together, toward the door to the boys' locker room.

"I'm Peter." He paused for a few seconds. "Pratt, huh? You're not by any chance related to *Chris* Pratt, are you?"

Chris nodded. "I sure am. Chris and Susan are my cousins."

"No kidding." He looked at her more carefully

68

than he had before. "Well, I guess you look *sort* of like the Pratt twins, a little bit, anyway . . . but not really."

It was all Chris could do to keep from laughing.

"So I guess you must know Chris pretty well, then, huh?"

Even though Peter Blake was apparently quite interested in discussing Christine Pratt, that was the last topic that Chris-as-Charlie wanted to discuss. "Yes, I guess I do. But let me ask you something. Did you ever wonder how come Mr. Nagle calls everybody by his last name?"

Peter just looked at her strangely.

Chris realized then that she had just asked a question that most boys would never ask. Why, it was not at all uncommon for boys to be called by their last names. Girls, on the other hand, tended to be addressed by their first names. Or else as "Miss," as in "Miss Pratt."

There's *another* difference, she noted with surprise. A small one, maybe, but it must mean something. As if teachers and everybody else feel they have to be more polite around girls. Treat them with more courtesy. As if we girls couldn't take being called by our last names! Now, *there's* something that makes no sense at all!

But Chris didn't have much time to dwell on her latest observation.

She and Peter had just entered the boys' locker room.

Fortunately, it was still early, and there weren't many boys there yet. The few that were there were taking their time, chatting with one another as they dialed the combinations to open their lockers. Even so, Chris kept her eyes down. She felt so out of place here! Yet she had to be careful not to let on. . . .

Peter led her to the back, where empty lockers were available. She thanked him. Then, just before racing toward the boys' room, where she could change out of the way of all the other boys, she said, "By the way, Peter, what sport have you been playing lately in gym class?"

Peter answered her question in a matter-of-fact tone. "Wrestling."

Chris gulped. Susan Pratt, she was thinking, wait until I get my hands on you!

The boys' room, she was relieved to discover, was empty. She changed quickly. Fortunately, the extra-large gym shorts hung down to her knees, and the huge Whittington High sweatshirt covered almost every other part of her body. When she glanced at her reflection in the mirror, she actually laughed.

She slunk through the locker room on her way out to the gym, once again keeping her eyes on the floor. She could hear all the boys in Mr. Nagle's third-period gym class, hooting and joking and tossing one another's sneakers around playfully.

So what if I can't be a "fly on the wall" in the boys' locker room! Chris thought as she shut the door firmly behind her. I can still observe what they're like during gym class, when there are no girls around.

Once she was out in the gym, Scott Stevens spotted her right away.

"Hey, Charlie!" he called, making his way over. "I didn't expect to see you here."

"Well, Chris has gym on her schedule this period, so I figured I'd take advantage of it to get some exercise myself."

"Good thing you didn't get stuck in the *girls'* gym class!" Scott joked. "You'd probably end up spending the whole period practicing giving tea parties!'

Chris was astounded by what Scott had just said. Not only was it unfair; it was so far from the truth that she couldn't believe she had actually heard him say it! She thought about all the female athletes that had helped Whittington High make a name for itself in high school sports. The girls' basketball team had won last year's county championship. Her friend Katy Johnson was a first-rate gymnast, good enough to pursue a career as a professional athlete. And even Chris Pratt was an accomplished competitive swimmer. Then there was the fact that all the girls' gym classes were demanding, just as the boys' were.

But this was not the time or place to start defending Whittington High's female students.

As it was, she didn't have a chance to say anything. Just then, Mr. Nagle blew his whistle and announced loudly, "All rights, boys. Let's get started. I'd like to take a break from our usual routine today. We'll go back to wrestling in a couple of weeks. For now, I'd like to start you guys on some gymnastics."

Chris was so relieved that she felt as if her knees had just melted. Good-bye, wrestling. Hello, gymnastics.

At the same time, however, she experienced a twinge of disappointment. All of a sudden, she felt like showing Scott Stevens that girls could handle *any* sport.

I'll just have to set him straight some other time, she thought. Hopefully, I'll have plenty of chances to do that in the future!

Mr. Nagle started out the period with ten minutes of

vigorous calisthenics. Being both a cheerleader and a member of Whittington High's girls' swimming team, Chris had very little trouble keeping up. She couldn't help being pleased by that. She hoped that Scott noticed how well Charlie Pratt was keeping up with the rest of the class . . . but of course it wouldn't even occur to him to check something like that out. Since Charlie was "one of the boys," Scott would just *assume* he was better at athletics than any girl could ever be!

As she launched energetically into push-ups, something else occurred to Chris.

Good thing it's me, and not Susan, who's pretending to be Charlie! She thought as she finished her twentieth push-up. She's not nearly in such good shape.

Chris resolved, then and there, to start encouraging her sister to get more exercise and to participate in sports more often. Not only would it be good for her; her twin was missing out on a lot of fun.

That's something that boys are geared toward all their lives, she thought. Girls are generally encouraged to do less-active things. Or even to stay on the sidelines, just watching, while boys have all the fun!

Why, come to think of it, there's even an element of that in cheerleading! The boys are playing, and the girls are *encouraging* them to play. And that's okay, except that now that I think about it, when we *girls* play basketball or participate in swim meets, there are no cheerleaders for *us*—either boys *or* girls!

Once again, Chris was amazed at how much the Marshmallow Masquerade was teaching her. She kept learning all kinds of things about the different ways

72

that boys and girls were treated—often ways that made no sense at all or else were based on really old-fashioned ideas.

From now on, she decided, I'm going to be more aware of those "differences" and what they mean!

For now, however, she had more pressing matters to deal with. Like how she was going to get through the rest of this gym class!

After the calisthenics workout, Mr. Nagle had the boys gather around the parallel bars. Chris was used to seeing the bars set up so that they were uneven, with one of them placed much higher than the other. In fact, it was on the uneven parallel bars that the female gymnasts had distinguished themselves at the last few Olympics.

Boys, however, used them differently. They were arranged so that both bars were lined up at the same level.

"Okay, boys," Mr. Nagle announced. "Today we're going to try a simple exercise, just to give you a chance to become familiar with this piece of equipment. What I want you to do is pull yourself up and, keeping your elbows stiff, use your arms to walk the length of the bars."

I can do that, Chris thought smugly.

"Okay, let's go in alphabetical order. Andrews, you're up first!"

One by one, the boys got up and tried the exercise on the parallel bars. Peter Blake did fine; Chris was surprised to find that she was actually rooting for him.

I guess it's because he was nice to me before. I mean, he was nice to *Charlie*.

When it was Chris's turn, she did just as well as all the others.

"Good going," said Mr. Nagle. And as she jumped down from the bars, several of the boys slapped her on the back.

This is easy! she thought proudly. I'm doing just as well as anybody else in this class!

When everyone had had a chance on the parallel bars, Mr. Nagle had the boys try a few other pieces of gymnastic equipment. The rings were a bit difficult for Chris, because they demanded real strength. She just thanked her lucky stars that she had been working hard on her Australian crawl lately, one of her favorite swimming strokes. She also managed to keep up with the boys on the horse and the horizontal bar.

By the end of the class, Chris was exhilarated.

I made it! she thought over and over again. I actually managed to participate in a boys' gym class without a single person suspecting that I wasn't just like everybody else in the class!

She couldn't wait to tell Susan.

Just as she had before, Chris changed her clothes in the boys' room, steering clear of the locker room. On her way out, however, she overheard some of the boys talking about Charlie Pratt.

"Hey, what about that new kid, Pratt?" jeered a voice she didn't recognize. "Pretty puny, don't you think?"

The next voice, however, was familiar to her. "Yeah, he's skinny, all right," said Scott Stevens. "At least I don't have to worry about him taking over as captain of the basketball team!"

Chris was bewildered. Was it possible that Scott actually felt competitive toward Charlie Pratt? The two boys hardly knew each other! Not to mention the fact that they were supposedly starting up a friendship. . . . It didn't make much sense.

Then again, ever since the Marshmallow Masquerade had begun, Chris had been finding out that a *lot* of things didn't make much sense!

She was even more surprised to hear another familiar voice rush to Charlie's defense.

"Aw, lay off," Peter Blake said. "He's an okay guy. So what if he's not as strong as you guys?"

Chris rushed out of the locker room then. It was getting late, and she had to hurry if she didn't want to be late for her next class.

But she was suddenly so confused! And not only about the things she was learning about boys and girls, either. Here she had thought that Scott Stevens was the best thing since chunky peanut butter, and she was discovering that there was another side to him, one that was much less attractive. On the other hand, Peter Blake, the school nerd, wasn't such a bad guy after all.

And it was all because she had started looking at them both as *equals,* instead of as separate, mysterious, *different* creatures. She was seeing them as people, instead of as boys that she might or might not like to date.

Whoa! thought Chris, shaking her head slowly. I thought that the Marshmallow Masquerade might be fun and that I might learn a few things. But I never, ever suspected that from now on I would start looking at everything differently!

Eight

As Chris followed Scott up the narrow path that led to the front door of the Stevenses' house later on that same afternoon, she was still feeling a bit over-whelmed by all that she was finding out simply by pretending to be Charlie Pratt. Even so, she was more enthusiastic than ever about the Marshmallow Masquerade. Why, here it was only Tuesday, yet she already felt as if she were the world's foremost expert on teenage boys!

And now she was on the verge of embarking upon still one more phase of this adventure. She was about to see where Scott lived, how he acted at home, and how he treated his friends. His *male* friends.

"Thanks for inviting me over, Scott," Chris-as-Charlie said as she stepped inside and looked around. It was a nice house, quite simple, but made comfort-able and warm by numerous small touches. There was a vase of fresh flowers on the coffee table in the living room, and the smell of freshly baked cookies was in the air. The dining room table was already set for dinner. Everything was neat and clean, from the shining wooden floors to the plumped-up pillows on the couch to the highly polished furniture. Chris could tell that a lot of work—and love—had gone into making this place a real home.

"Anybody here?" Scott called as he walked in, depositing his schoolbooks and jacket on the nearest table.

His mother immediately came in from the kitchen. "Hello, dear. Oh, I see you've brought a friend home with you. How nice!"

"Mom, this is Charlie Pratt. He's the cousin of some girls I know at school. He's visiting from Chicago, just for the week."

"Hello, Mrs. Stevens," Chris-as-Charlie said politely. "I'm pleased to meet you."

"I'm pleased to meet you, too, Charlie. Would you boys like a snack? I just baked some cookies—"

"What kind?" Scott interrupted her.

"Chocolate chip."

"Aw, Mom, not again! You *always* make that kind!" Scott, Chris was astonished to see, was practically pouting.

"I'd love a cookie, Mrs. Stevens," Charlie ventured. "My mother hardly ever finds the time to bake."

She was about to add, "My sister and I love to whip up a batch of cookies or a cake on a rainy Saturday afternoon," but stopped herself. She had forgotten, for a moment, who she was supposed to be. And while a comment like that would have passed virtually unnoticed if Chris said it, having *Charlie,* a seventeen-year-old boy, say the exact same thing was practically guaranteed to attract a lot of attention.

"Are Paul and Ted home yet?" asked Scott as he headed for the kitchen. "They're my younger brothers," he explained to Charlie.

"I just picked them up at the junior high. Paul had a Boy Scout meeting to go to, and so I dropped Ted off in the same neighborhood, at his friend Larry's house. Oh, I also picked up your suit at the dry cleaners, Scott."

Mrs. Stevens accompanied her son and his guest into the kitchen. Even though it was apparent from the pile of vegetables on the wooden cutting board near the sink that she had been busy preparing dinner, she proceeded to fill two glasses with milk and arrange some of the cookies, still warm from the oven, on a plate.

She was getting some paper napkins down from a shelf when Chris said, "That's okay, Mrs. Stevens. You don't have to do all this. We can just help ourselves."

Scott looked at his new friend strangely.

"Oh, that's all right," Mrs. Stevens said cheerfully. "You boys have put in a long day at school. You deserve a break."

Just then, the telephone rang. "Excuse me a minute, boys. I'll just answer that upstairs. Then I'll be out of your way. . . ."

When she was gone, Chris observed, "Gee, Scott, it's awfully nice that your mother bakes homemade cookies for your family."

"Well, why not? She's got nothing else to do all day! I mean, she doesn't work or anything."

Chris was astonished. Mrs. Stevens, *not work*?

How on earth could Scott ever come up with a comment like that? It was obvious she had just spent the entire day cleaning the house, running errands, picking up Scott's two younger brothers and driving them to their friends' houses, starting dinner, setting the table . . . not to mention baking cookies!

And yet Scott didn't notice any of that at all. It was as if he just *expected* all those things to get done, without ever taking the time to realize that *someone* had to spend time and energy *doing* them! And that someone was his mother.

A minute later Mrs. Stevens stuck her head through the kitchen doorway. "Are you boys all right in here?" she asked. "Is there anything else you need?"

"We're fine, Mom," Scott said, scowling.

"Aren't you going to sit down and have a snack with us, Mrs. Stevens?" Chris asked.

This time, the look that Scott cast in her direction was one of disbelief.

"Why, thank you, Charlie! That's very nice of you. But Scott doesn't want his *mother* around while he's talking to his friends!" And she was gone.

Chris was bewildered. It was growing increasingly obvious to her that Mrs. Stevens wasn't treated very well in her own home. In fact, it even appeared that she didn't *expect* to! Everything she did for her family was taken for granted—at least by her oldest son. She wasn't even welcome to sit down with him for a few minutes after school, to talk about the day and meet his new friend!

Of course, Chris reminded herself, all teenagers want time away from their parents, especially when their friends are around. Even Sooz and I, who really enjoy spending time with Mom, talking and laughing and introducing our friends to her, are always holing up in our bedrooms to discuss this boy or that teacher . . . or our current prank. But Scott is being positively *rude*!

There was something else troubling Chris. The way Scott acted toward his mother seemed to have something to do with the comment he'd made earlier that afternoon about the girls' gym classes. Saying that the girls probably spent the period . . . What was it? "Practicing giving tea parties." They both reflected the same attitude.

And, Chris was realizing, it was an attitude she didn't like very much at all.

Come on, Chris, you're being too critical, she argued with herself. Scott's just showing off. Don't be in such a hurry to find fault with him! After all, this is your big chance to find out what he's *really* like!

Even so, Chris couldn't help feeling more and more uncomfortable. Maybe this *was* what Scott Stevens was "really like."

"So, Charlie, how do you like Whittington High so far?"

"Well, it's okay, I guess. It's, uh, a lot different from my school."

"Yeah, I bet. Coming from a big city like Chicago and all." Scott had already wolfed down at least a dozen cookies. Chris was just about to bite into her second.

Uh-oh. I'd better start gobbling these cookies down, she thought ruefully. Otherwise, Scott might get suspicious.

She stuck the whole cookie into her mouth, all at once, wondering if she would ever fit into her favorite pair of jeans again.

"I guess the kids in Chicago must be pretty different from the way they are in a small town like Whittington," Scott went on.

"No, not really." Chris recognized this as an opportunity to steer the conversation toward the topic of girls. And once they started talking about girls, she could bring up the subject of Charlie's cousin Chris once again. "What are the girls like at Whittington High?" she asked, trying to sound casual.

"Most of them are okay. A lot of them are much too independent, though."

Chris blinked. "Independent?"

"Yeah, you know. Trying too hard to . . . well, to be like boys."

"What do you mean, exactly?"

"Oh, signing up for Shop class, or even Mechanical Drawing, instead of sticking to Cooking and Sewing, the way they should. Insisting upon using the gym for stupid sports like girls' basketball, when we guys could be using it.

"You know, some of them have even started asking guys out! There's this one girl I know, Katy Johnson. A couple of weeks ago, she actually called up this boy named Wayne and invited him to the Halloween Dance!"

"Gee," Chris-as-Charlie said meekly, "what's wrong with that?"

Scott looked at his new friend Charlie as if he had just sprouted three more heads. "Girls just aren't supposed to *do* things like that, that's all!"

Chris was debating whether she should continue to try to find out more about Scott's way of thinking or just drop the whole subject before he became suspicious, when Scott said, "Hey, why don't we go up to my room? I'll show you my basketball trophy. I won it last year, for being the most outstanding player in the county's high school basketball league."

She tried to look impressed. "Wow. Sure."

While Chris wasn't particularly interested in looking at some boring old trophy, she was looking forward to seeing Scott's room. Hopefully, it would help her get an even clearer glimpse of what Scott Stevens was really like.

Scott's room was a mess. While someone had made an effort to decorate it nicely at one point, painting it a pleasant shade of light blue, putting up attractive blue and yellow plaid curtains made out of the same fabric as the bedspread, and choosing two or three scatter rugs that picked up the colors in the fabric, there was so much clutter that those efforts had been in vain.

There were clothes everywhere, draped across the chair, rolled up in balls and stashed on the dresser, even lying on the floor. Books were stuck on shelves haphazardly, and sporting equipment was strewn around randomly. There were even a few candy wrappers and an empty soda can sitting on the desk, forgotten.

"Gee," Chris gulped. "This is . . . quite a room."

"Yeah, my folks let me keep it the way I want it." Scott sounded almost proud. "My mom doesn't even come in here anymore, except to change the sheets." He plopped down on the bed without taking off his sneakers.

"Hey, there's the trophy I was telling you about." He gestured toward the bookcase in one corner of the room. Sure enough, it was displayed proudly on the very top shelf. "Pretty neat, huh?"

"Great." Chris no longer knew what she was doing here. She had hoped to find out what Scott Stevens was really like. Yet from what she'd learned in just the past few minutes, she was beginning to wonder why she had ever even *cared* in the first place!

She was trying to think up an excuse to getting out of there when she heard Mrs. Stevens call upstairs, "Scott! Hank is here! Shall I send him up?"

"Hey, terrific! Do you know Hank Griffith?"

Chris shook her head. Actually, she and Hank had been in school together ever since kindergarten. But, of course, that was *Chris* and Hank, not *Charlie* and Hank.

A few seconds later Hank came bounding into Scott's room.

"Hey Scott! How's it going?" Hank greeted his friend energetically. He noticed Charlie then, sitting on the floor. He nodded over in his direction.

"Hiya, Hank. Listen, this is Charlie Pratt. He's Chris and Susan Pratt's cousin, visiting from Chicago."

Like Scott, Hank was on Whittington High's basketball team. As she shook hands with him, her heart sank. Mike Anderson's suggestion that the two of them shoot some baskets together suddenly came back to her. What if the same idea occurred to these two basketball heroes?

Fortunately, Scott and Hank felt more like listening to records than playing basketball today. Hank turned on the stereo and plopped down on the floor beside Charlie.

"So, you're Susan Pratt's cousin, huh?" he asked congenially.

"Yup."

"You know, I've always thought that Susan was pretty cool. Yeah, I might even ask her out one of these days. Who knows? Maybe I'll ask her to the Homecoming Dance."

Chris opened her mouth to protest . . . but remembered that Charlie Pratt would have no way of knowing that Hank was supposedly going out with Holly Anderson. That Holly, in fact, was hoping—expecting, even—that Hank would invite *her* to the Homecoming Dance!

Well, it's now or never, thought Chris. If I want to find out what these boys really think of the girls I know, I'd better start asking some direct questions.

"Gee, isn't that Homecoming Dance this weekend?" Charlie asked innocently. "I'm surprised you haven't already asked somebody, Hank. You're not . . . going out with anybody right now?"

"Well, sort of. I mean, there's this one girl, Holly Anderson. . . . In fact, I think she's friends with your cousin Chris. We went out a couple of weeks ago. . . ."

"So why don't you go to the dance with her?" Charlie suggested bravely. She could tell that Hank was more than eager to talk about his social life, so any hesitation she might have felt about discussing it with him vanished.

"Maybe she told him to buzz off after the first date!" Scott joked. He was still lounging on the bed with his arms crossed behind his head.

"So your date with—what's her name, Holly?— didn't go too well, huh?" asked Charlie.

"Oh, I don't know. I mean, it was okay. But, well, I'm not sure if she really likes me."

Of *course* she likes you! Chris was tempted to

scream. But she couldn't. So, instead, she said calmly, "How come?"

Hank shrugged. "She was acting kind of . . . distant. On our date, I mean."

Scott laughed. "You mean she didn't want to kiss you!"

Hank was turning pink. Even though Scott was teasing him, however, he remained eager to tell Charlie all about his date with Holly.

Probably because he doesn't have anyone else to talk to, Chris thought. Especially if all his friends are like Scott!

"Yeah, well, that's kind of what happened."

"But that's crazy!" Chris cried. This time, she forgot all about the fact that she was supposed to be Charlie. "Just because she didn't want to kiss you doesn't mean she doesn't like you! Maybe she just doesn't like to kiss boys she doesn't really know!"

Hank looked startled. "Hey, you know I never thought of that," he said. He was quiet for a few seconds, as if he was pondering this new idea.

"Oh, why don't you call her and ask her to the dance," Chris said offhandedly, once again remembering who she was. "What have you got to lose?"

"What has he got to lose?" Scott demanded with a snort. "Well, she might turn him down, for one thing!"

What would be so terrible about that? Chris wondered.

But she thought for a second. If she were a boy, she decided, she would also find it a little scary to call up a girl and ask her out—especially if it was hard to tell what the girl's feelings were. The idea of calling a boy always seemed so terrifying to her . . . and she realized, for the first time, that it probably wasn't very much easier for boys to call girls! So what if it was much more acceptable? They still ran the risk of being rejected. And no one, boys or girls, wanted to go through that!

My dear twin Susan, she thought with a sigh, you've hit it on the head, once again.

But for the moment, she wanted to help Hank out. It was funny; up until now, she had been annoyed with him for "ignoring" Holly. And now she was seeing things from his side, finding out that he had been thinking the exact same thing as her girlfriend: that *Holly* didn't really like *him*!

"So call her," Chris-as-Charlie suggested one more time.

"Maybe I will," said Hank. "Yeah, now that I think about it, I guess it's not such a bad idea, after all."

While they were on the subject of the girls they knew, Chris decided to push things just a little bit further. "Hey, do either of you guys know Beth Thompson? She's a friend of my cousin Susan's. I was, uh, thinking of asking her out."

"Are you kidding?" Scott whooped. "You want to ask 'Princess Beth' out? Hah! She's so stuck-up, she probably wouldn't even *lower* herself to talk to you!"

Beth isn't stuck-up! Chris thought with surprise. She's just shy!

But she realized immediately that Beth's inability to relax with boys, to chat with them and joke with them, was interpreted by them as snobbery. When she ran away from them because she was so self-conscious around boys, they just assumed she thought she was "too good for them."

Wow, wait until I talk to Beth, thought Chris.

But then she realized that she couldn't just go up to her and say, "Guess what I found out, Beth!"

Yet there had to be some way of letting her know what boys really thought of her, that they were put off not because of her shyness but because they thought *she* didn't like *them*. . . .

More miscommunication! Chris shook her head slowly as she pondered all the situations she had already run into in which great misunderstandings arose between boys and girls just because it was so difficult for them both just to *be themselves* around each other. They were always trying to figure each other out, to second-guess every word and action. There was so much emphasis on the *differences* between them that sometimes the *similarities* got lost!

By that point, it was getting late. Chris was surprised when she glanced at the clock on Scott's desk, almost hidden by a candy wrapper, and saw that it was getting close to dinnertime. In a way, she didn't want to tear herself away from this conversation with Hank and Scott. She was learning so much! Not only about them and her friends . . . but also the way boys thought. About themselves *and* about girls. There was so much she wanted to discuss with Susan that she felt as if she were about to burst.

"Listen, guys, I'd better get going," Chris said, standing up and heading toward the door. "I promised my, uh, aunt that I'd help her with some things."

"Okay, Charlie. See you around school," said Hank with a wave.

"Yeah, Charlie," Scott added. "See you. Hey, and thanks for coming over. We'll have to do it again sometime soon. You know, I really enjoyed getting to know you a little better."

"Yeah," Chris agreed, smiling to herself as she walked out the door of Scott's bedroom. "I really enjoyed getting to know *you* better, too."

Nine

"Christine Pratt! What on earth are you doing?"

It was Tuesday evening, just before dinner, and Susan had just come into her sister's room, anxious to hear all the details of day two of the Marshmallow Masquerade. She expected to find Chris sitting at her desk, doing her homework, or sprawled across her bed, reading or listening to music.

Instead, she was flat on the floor, dressed in an old Whittington High T-shirt and a pair of turquoise sweat pants, doing push-ups. All around her were pieces of gym equipment—barbells, dumbbells, even a stopwatch—that had undoubtedly been retrieved from the attic. Chris's face was flushed bright red from exertion, and little beads of perspiration had collected on her forehead.

It was obvious to Susan that her twin had just undertaken a body-building program. And, as in the case of everything else, Chris was throwing herself into it wholeheartedly.

After her initial surprise, it occurred to Susan that Chris's sudden determination to become physically fit had to have something to do with the Marshmallow Masquerade.

"Oh, *I* know," she said, answering her own question. "You've decided that you can make a much more convincing boy if you're more muscular . . . right?"

"You're getting warm," Chris puffed. She stopped doing push-ups and plopped down on the floor, sitting cross-legged. "Susan, after giving the Marshmallow Masquerade a lot of thought, I've come to a decision. A *major* decision. One I hope you'll back me up on."

Susan was immediately filled with doubt. She had no idea what was coming, but she had seen that look in her twin sister's eyes before, and she knew what it meant. "I'm not about to make any promises, Chris. . . ."

"Sooz, I've decided that there's only one thing to do." She paused dramatically. "Charlie Pratt has got to fight Eddie McKay this Friday."

Susan's mouth dropped open. "Chris, you've *got* to be kidding! I mean, you don't really expect—"

"Listen to me. Just for a minute. Please." With great difficulty, Chris pulled herself up off the floor. She staggered over to her bed and sprawled across it. Still huffing and puffing, still flushed beet red, she lay there for a few seconds, totally limp.

Someone's going to ache all over tomorrow, Susan thought sympathetically.

"When you and I agreed to go ahead with the Marshmallow Masquerade," Chris began once she'd caught her breath, "we intended to do it *right*. One hundred percent. The plan was that I would pretend to

90

be a teenage boy so that we could find out what it was really like to be a teenage boy. Remember?"

"Yes, but—"

"Well, I've learned quite a bit in the past two days. More than I ever expected, in fact. And one of the things I've learned is that boys are expected to be tough. To fight. It stinks, I'll admit, and I certainly don't approve of it. But it's a fact."

"Yes, I know. Even so, Chris—"

"If I really were Charlie Pratt—which, for all intents and purposes, I am—I wouldn't be able to run away or hide, the way I could if I were Chris Pratt just pretending to be a boy. I have to do everything that Charlie would do; otherwise, the entire Marshmallow Masquerade is nothing but a . . . a . . . big *game*.

"Either we're going to take it seriously or we might as well call the whole thing off. Just end it right now and consider it a failure. Something that the Pratt twins just weren't up to carrying through."

Susan was about to protest one more time. She opened her mouth, but no words came out. Finally, she said, "I hate to admit it, Chris, but you've got a point there. If you're going to be Charlie Pratt, you've got to be him one hundred percent. Not only as far as it's fun or convenient . . . or safe."

Suddenly she slapped herself on the forehead. "For goodness' sake! What am I *saying*? Surely you don't expect me to say, 'Gee, Chris, you're right. Go ahead and have it out with Eddie after school on Friday.' *Do* you?"

Chris sat up, now back to her usual energetic self. "Susan, given the situation, I don't see how you could possibly say anything *but* that!"

"Hey, wait a minute. This doesn't happen to have

anything to do with Scott Stevens, does it? Did something happen while you were at his house?"

Chris thought for a few seconds. "Well . . . yes and no. Let's just say that I'm more determined than ever to make the Marshmallow Masquerade work. And not only to learn about what it's like to be a teenage boy, either. I also want to prove—to myself, at least—that I can do anything that a teenage boy can do! And if that means I have to fight the school bully, well, then, I'll just have to go ahead and fight the school bully!"

Susan sighed and shook her head slowly. "Look, I understand the point you're trying to make. And I'm with you completely. At least in theory. But you're not talking about learning what it's like to be a boy. You're talking about black eyes and . . . and bloody noses. Maybe even *broken* noses! Just think, Chris. If you got your nose broken, you and I wouldn't be identical twins anymore!"

"We're not identical *now,* Sooz. Not since I got my hair cut!"

"Christine Pratt, that's the very least of it, and you know it. For heaven's sake, you could get a broken arm or a fractured jaw, or . . ."

With great seriousness, Chris replied, "Apparently all that is part of being a boy."

"But not *every* boy has to have a fight with the school bully!"

"No, not every boy. But *this* boy does. Charlie Pratt has gotten into a situation where he has to fight. It's expected of him, and there's no way out."

Slowly Chris climbed off the bed. She picked up two ten-pound dumbbells, one in each hand, and rhythmically began to lift them. Up, down, up, down.

Susan just looked on, totally at a loss as to what to say to her twin.

I know Chris is stubborn, she was thinking, or at least that once she's committed to something, she carries it through all the way. And there's no reason why the Marshmallow Masquerade should be any different. . . .

Even so, the mere thought of her twin sister having a fist fight with Eddie McKay filled her with fear. Why, not only was he the school bully; he probably weighed at least one-and-a-half times what Chris weighed! Not to mention the fact that he was considerably stronger than she was, simply because he was a boy.

No, she couldn't let this happen. She would have to come up with some idea, think of some way to talk Chris out of this brand-new resolution of hers. The whole thing was crazy, totally impossible.

Why, then, Susan wondered as she stood in the doorway of her sister's room, watching her pant and strain as she lifted her dumbbells one more time, was she actually feeling *proud* of her twin sister?

The next morning, Chris was still determined to follow through on her commitment to playing the role of Charlie Pratt by taking on Eddie McKay. But the upcoming fight wasn't until Friday. Today was only Wednesday, and so she stashed it away at the back of her mind. For the moment, she had other things to concentrate on—like day three of the Marshmallow Masquerade.

"What's on for today, Chris—oops, I mean, Charlie?" Mr. Pratt teased over breakfast. "Funny, it's hard for me to get used to the idea of having a young man in the house after seventeen years of being the father of twin daughters!"

Chris laughed. "Well, don't get *too* used to it. Charlie's only going to be in town until Saturday. As for your question about what's on for today, well, things should be relatively calm."

Her mother's eyebrows shot up. " 'Calm'? Since when can going around school pretending to be a boy be described as *calm*?"

"I guess I'm getting used to it," Chris said with a chuckle. "I'm actually beginning to feel comfortable as Charlie. But when I said today would be calm, what I meant was, there's no gym class, no visit to Scott Stevens's house. No, today should be fairly routine. The only thing that's new for Charlie today is study hall."

Her twin glanced at the kitchen clock. "Well, Chris or Charlie or whoever you are, we'd better get moving or we'll be late for school."

"Okay, Sooz. In a second. First I want to clear the table and put away the milk and the butter."

The other three Pratts stared at Chris in disbelief.

"Why, Chris!" Mrs. Pratt exclaimed. "You're always the first one to leave the table! You go shooting out of here every morning, suddenly realizing that if you don't hurry, you'll never make it to school on time."

"I know. But I want to start carrying my weight around here. It's not fair for Mom to get stuck doing *everything,* you know!"

"Well, I can't say I understand it," Mr. Pratt remarked, "but it seems to me that the Marshmallow Masquerade is teaching our Chris about a *lot* of things!"

"I don't understand it either," said Mrs. Pratt. "But I'm certain of one thing: I *like* it!"

Just as Chris had predicted, day three started out uneventfully. With the exception of Eddie McKay and his friends, who once again went out of their way to be menacing during homeroom, the students of Whittington High had by now simply accepted Charlie Pratt, paying him no more and no less attention than they did anyone else. Chris drifted through the day, positively smug about how smoothly things were going.

That is, until fourth-period study hall.

It was the last place in the world that Chris would have expected to run into trouble. As a matter of fact, she had actually been looking forward to it. Certainly, she would get a chance to concentrate on getting part of her homework done. But she would also have some time to relax. Despite her increasing confidence about the Marshmallow Masquerade, it was still a bit tiring, constantly having to remember to use a deeper voice, to sit and walk and move differently, to avoid entirely some expressions and some topics of conversation.

Chris immediately headed for a seat in the back of the large room in which study halls were held, hoping for some peace and quiet so she could tackle the essay on poetry that had just been assigned that morning in English class. Of course, she would pretend that the ailing and bedridden Chris had actually written it, that Charlie had merely told her about the assignment.

Too bad Charlie *isn't* real, she thought with a sigh as she stared at the blank sheet of paper in front of her, trying to think of a topic. Maybe he'd be able to give me some help with this essay, since I haven't got a single idea.

It was then that she noticed the two girls who were

sitting in front of her. Jane Waters and Lisa Green were giggling and whispering and passing notes—all three of which were not allowed during study hall. Chris was just about to ask them to keep it down so she could concentrate on her homework when the teacher who was conducting study hall that day, Ms. Simmons, scolded them, "There is not talking during study hall! Please keep it down back there!"

Jane and Lisa looked at each other and smirked, and Chris turned back to her essay. But before she had even had the chance to write down the title "The Poems of Emily Dickinson," she heard the talking and laughing start up again.

"Excuse me!" called out Ms. Simmons, sounding even more annoyed. "Just because you're sitting at the back of the room doesn't mean I can't hear you! I suggest you get busy with some schoolwork before I start sending some of you down to the principal's office!"

Dramatically, Lisa rolled her eyes upward. Jane acted as if that were the funniest thing she had ever seen in her life. With her hands clapped over her mouth, she stifled another giggle.

Chris just shook her head slowly and went back to her essay. But as she started to write the first sentence, she suddenly felt something graze her cheek. Surprised, she glanced up and saw a paper airplane land on the floor next to her desk. She was about to say something to Lisa and Jane . . . but when she looked over at them, they both had their noses buried in their textbooks, looking so innocent and so involved in what they were doing that no one would have ever guessed that they were the ones who were responsible for all the commotion.

No one, including Ms. Simmons. She was hurrying down the aisle, toward the back of the room. But she bypassed Lisa and Jane completely. Instead, it was in front of Charlie Pratt's desk that she stopped.

"Young man, what do you think you're doing, disrupting this entire study hall?"

At first, Chris was too astonished to speak. "But . . . I . . ." she sputtered.

"Didn't you hear me *ask* you to stop talking and passing notes? *Didn't* you?"

"Well, yes, but it wasn't me—"

"You teenage boys are such troublemakers! You all think that school is some kind of joke. Well, Mr. Know-It-All, I'm going to show you once and for all that you boys can't get away with such shenanigans. *You*, young man, are going right down to the principal's office!"

Chris's heart sank. She had never been sent to the principal's office in her life! And now not only was she in real trouble; it was for something she hadn't even done! Even though two girls who were sitting in the back of the room were the ones disobeying the rules, Ms. Simmons just *assumed* that one of the boys was responsible.

And then she realized that being sent to the principal's office was going to be even more difficult because she wasn't really a boy! What if he started asking questions about who Charlie was . . . or, worse yet, tried to get in touch with Charlie Pratt's high school in Chicago?

Chris was in a panic. She didn't know what to do. She had to get out of this some way, but she couldn't decide upon the best way to handle it.

And then, all of a sudden, she heard someone

beside her say, "It wasn't Charlie here who was responsible, Ms. Simmons. It was somebody else. And I'd be willing to go along to the principal's office to tell my side of the story, if you don't believe me."

Even before she turned to look, Chris knew whose voice that was.

"Thanks, Peter," she said softly. "Peter is right, Ms. Simmons. It wasn't me."

"Hmph," said Ms. Simmons indignantly. But with Peter Blake as a witness, she could no longer accuse Charlie Pratt of doing something he hadn't done. She looked around, her eyes lighting for a split second on Jane and Lisa, who were still pretending to be absorbed in their reading. "Well, let me just warn all of you that I'm serious. I insist upon silence in this study hall!" With that, she stomped back up to the front of the room.

It wasn't until the end of fourth period that Chris had a chance to go over to Peter and thank him.

"Wow, I really appreciate the way you went out on a limb for me," she said sincerely. "If you hadn't spoken up, I would have had to go to the principal's office!"

Peter shrugged. "I was just doing the right thing, Charlie. I would have done it for anybody. Although," he added teasingly, "the fact that you're Chris Pratt's cousin *may* have had something to do with it. Maybe I can get you to put in a good word for me now!"

"Hey, Peter, want to have lunch together?" called Dennis Barker, Peter Blake's best friend—and, Chris had always thought, just another "nerd."

"Sure, Dennis. Wait up." Peter turned back to Charlie. "How about you, Charlie? Do you have lunch fifth period?"

"Yes . . ."

"Great! Want to sit with us?"

Chris hesitated. Her first reaction was "Oh, no! Eating lunch with two *nerds*?" But then she remembered that Peter had just bailed her out of what could have become a very unpleasant situation. And that just the day before, he had gone out of his way to befriend "the new boy" in gym class—and to defend him when Scott Stevens and some of the others were making fun of him. Peter Blake wasn't a "nerd"; he was a friendly, caring person.

And I never would have found that out if it weren't for the Marshmallow Masquerade, thought Chris.

"Peter," Chris-as-Charlie said, patting him on the back, "I would be *honored* to have lunch with you and Dennis!"

And she really meant it.

The three of them bought their lunches and sat down together. Chris was surprised that when Scott Stevens came into the cafeteria, he simply glanced in their direction, then looked away, pretending he hadn't noticed Charlie and his new friends.

Fortunately, Peter and Dennis didn't notice. They were too busy trying to make Charlie Pratt feel at home.

"So, Charlie," Peter said in a friendly manner, "have you seen very much of Whittington?"

"Not really," Chris-as-Charlie returned. "I've been so busy filling in for Chris at school and all that I haven't really had much of a chance. What is there to see?"

"Well, there's a terrific monument in our town park that was just put up last summer. And then there's the town itself. If you like books, you should check out

Peterson's bookstore. And if you like ice cream, you should *definitely* try Fozzy's!"

Chris chuckled. "Fozzy's is a place I'm already very familiar with."

"Well, here's something I bet you never heard of," Dennis went on. "You should go see the Peter Blake Zoo."

Peter looked up from the peanut butter sandwich he was eating and blushed. "Aw, come on, Dennis."

"No, I'm serious. You see, Peter here has a real knack with animals. Taking care of them, I mean. He's always finding dogs and cats and birds that are sick or hurt and fixing them up so that they're good as new. The only trouble is," he added with a teasing grin, "he gets so attached to them that he can't bear the thought of giving them away. So instead, he keeps them all as pets!"

"Well, it's not as if we didn't have a big yard," Peter explained. "Besides, both my folks love animals almost as much as I do." Even though he was still beet red, it was apparent that he was flattered by his friend's enthusiastic report.

"That's really something, Peter," Chris said. "You mean you can actually cure sick animals?"

Dennis answered for him. "Oh, sure," he boasted. "He's really amazing. Peter's got this dog he found a few months ago. She was half starved, and covered with bruises. No one thought she was going to make it. But boy, you should see Ginger now! She's as rambunctious as any dog you'll ever meet! Then there's Cleopatra, this really beautiful cat, who had gotten hit by a car. Peter made a little splint and set her broken leg . . . and now she chases Ginger around the house as if she owned the place!"

Chris looked over at Peter with new admiration. "That's really something, Peter. Have you ever thought of becoming an animal doctor?"

"As a matter of fact, I have," he replied bashfully. "That's been my dream ever since I was a little kid. I've always planned to be a veterinarian one day."

"Well, you'll be a great vet, Peter," said Dennis. "You just have to get used to the idea that once you've finished taking care of all your patients, you've got to let them go back home with their owners!" He chuckled. "But seriously, Charlie, you should go over to Peter's house and see all the animals he's got. Rabbits, guinea pigs . . . even a raccoon."

"That sounds like some menagerie," said Chris. "And I'm amazed that you've taken such good care of them. I can't wait to see the 'Peter Blake Zoo.'"

"Really? You mean it?" Peter was flattered—not to mention surprised—that this "new boy," Christine Pratt's cousin, was actually interested in seeing his animals and hearing about how he'd brought so many of them back to good health.

"Sure," said Chris. "I'd really enjoy it. You know, I really like animals."

And, she noted with surprise as she bit into her tuna fish sandwich, I'm discovering that I kind of like Peter Blake, as well!

Ten

Even as Chris headed over to Peter Blake's house, that same afternoon, she found herself wondering what on earth she was doing. A week earlier, the mere thought of the popular, outgoing Christine Pratt going to visit the school nerd would have thrown her and her friends into fits of hysterical laughter. Yet here she was, not only on her way, but actually looking forward to it.

Not only because she loved animals, either.

It was a good thing she did, however. The moment she stepped inside the Blakes' house, she saw signs of Peter's hobby.

Immediately two dogs came bounding up to the front door, racing over from different parts of the house as soon as they heard Peter come in. And he was ready for them.

"Hey, Ginger! Hello, Waffles!" he cried as they both skidded toward him, then jumped up to lick his face, their tails wagging furiously. Peter gave them an equally enthusiastic greeting. He knelt down to hug them and scratch them behind the ears. "How's my girl? How's my fella?"

Chris's presence was also acknowledged by the friendly dogs. She bent over to pat them both as Peter introduced them proudly. Ginger, the dog that Dennis had been talking about, was a large reddish-blond dog, a mixed breed that was part Irish setter. She was still a bit thin, and there were marks where the bruises that Dennis mentioned had been. But she was otherwise a healthy animal. Waffles was much smaller, a light brown dog with long thick fur that made her look like a teddy bear. Even though both dogs were very different, it was obvious that they had one thing in common: they both adored their master.

A few seconds later, a sleek black cat leaped gracefully off the rocking chair in the living room, where she had been taking an afternoon nap. Chris knew immediately that she was Cleopatra, since she limped ever so slightly as she strolled over to Peter. As she rubbed herself against Peter's leg, purring a hello, he leaned over to stroke her fur.

"Hi there, Cleo," he said in a soft, friendly voice. "How's that leg of yours today?"

"Wow, this really is like a zoo!" Chris joked.

Secretly, however, she was more impressed with Peter Blake than ever. She could tell that these animals had been through some hard times. And that they were fully aware that it was Peter who had helped them through them.

"Wait until you see the menagerie I've got out back," Peter said with a wide grin. "This, I'm afraid, is just the beginning."

From the back of the house came sounds of a kettle boiling.

"Oh, good. My mother's home. I'd like you to meet her."

He gave each of the animals one final pat, then headed through the hallway, toward the kitchen. Not surprisingly, both dogs followed, not wanting to leave their master's side now that he was home.

"Hi, Mom! I'd like you to meet a new friend of mine, Charlie Pratt, from Chicago. He's visiting his cousins here in Whittington this week."

Peter's mother was sitting at the kitchen table, stirring sugar into the hot cup of tea she had just made for herself. "Hello, Charlie. I'm glad to meet you."

Chris half expected Peter to retreat from the kitchen, into his bedroom, immediately. Instead, he sat down next to his mother.

"How did your day go, Mom?"

"Oh, fine. I spent most of it at the library, researching that big paper I've been working on for the past few weeks. As a matter of fact, I just got home myself."

"My mom's working on her master's degree in social work," Peter said proudly. "And she's the smartest student at the whole university!"

"Oh, Peter," Ms. Blake laughed. "I wish that really were the case!"

"Aw, come on, Mom. You know you deserve a lot of credit for even going back to school in the first place!"

The three of them chatted for a while about Ms. Blake's courses and Peter's day at school. Then Peter said, "Well, we'll leave you alone so you can get some more work done on that paper. I'll start dinner in a couple of hours, Mom. I know you probably have a lot of notes to organize, if you were in the library all day. Oh, and don't forget that it's Dad's turn to set the table tonight. I'll remind him when he gets home, just in case he forgot."

Peter then turned to Charlie and said, "Let's give my mom some peace and quiet. I want to show you something outside, anyway. Hey, would you like an apple?"

Chris was dumbfounded as she followed Peter out of the kitchen after he'd picked out two bright, shining apples from the refrigerator. She was wondering how she could get Scott Stevens to come over to Peter's house when he said, "Boy, my mother is sure working hard these days. I really admire her for going back to school. Sure, my dad and my younger sister and I have to pitch in and do a lot more around the house, but we all agree that it's worth it if that's what makes Mom happy!"

Peter led Charlie out to a small shed in the Blakes' backyard. At one time, he explained, it had been used to store tools. Little by little, however, it had been converted into Dr. Blake's animal hospital.

"Fortunately, the walls of this place are thicker than you'd expect, so it doesn't get too cold in here," he said as he opened the door.

Inside the single tiny room, there were numerous cages, each one clean and spacious and equipped with bowls of water, food, and toys. And in each one there was at least one animal. In one of the cages was a white rabbit; in another, three guinea pigs. And sure enough, just as Dennis had said, one of the cages housed a chubby raccoon happily nibbling on a cookie. All in all, there were over a dozen small animals living in the shed.

"Wow, this really *is* a zoo!" said Chris, her voice filled with admiration. "Were all of these animals sick when you found them?"

"No, not all of them. But it's funny: animals who need homes just manage to find me somehow. A friend of mine who was moving away gave me these guinea pigs; the rabbit belonged to someone my parents know. . . . But the raccoon here, he just showed up on my doorstep one day with his eye in pretty bad shape. It looked as if he'd been in a fight, and he'd been hurt pretty badly. So . . . well, let's just say I did what I could for him."

Chris looked at the black and gray animal more closely. Sure enough, his left eye was red and swollen. Even so, it definitely looked as if he was on the road to recovery.

"Gee, Peter, you really do have a way with animals!" said Chris, looking at all of his pets one by one. And then an odd thought occurred to her.

"Can I ask you something, Peter?" Suddenly shy, she picked up a carrot she found lying next to one of the cages and began feeding it to the white rabbit.

"Sure. What?"

"What does it mean to you to be a boy?"

Peter looked over at his new friend in astonishment. "Boy, Charlie! You sure come up with some weird questions!"

"Well, uh, what I mean is, staying at my cousins' house has been making me think about the differences between them and me. After all, all three of us are about the same age, but . . . well, *you* know, Girls can be so *strange* sometimes! Know what I mean?"

Peter still looked puzzled. "I don't think girls are strange, Charlie. Oh, sure, they're different in some ways. But then again, think about all the other boys you know, and how different they all are from each other. Some of them love to watch football on TV. Others, like me, can't stand it."

"Really?"

"Oh, sure. I'd much rather play chess. Or read a book. Especially one about animals."

Chris thought for a minute. "Don't you ever feel pressured to do the things that boys are, well, 'supposed' to do? Like watching football, for example."

"Of course. Don't you?"

"Well . . . yes, I guess so."

"Fortunately, my folks aren't all wrapped up in having their son 'prove' anything. They don't care if I'm on the football team or not." Peter shrugged. "They just want me to be myself. To find what makes me happy and just do it, without worrying about what anybody else thinks."

Chris gulped. Here she had been thinking of Peter Blake as a nerd for as long as she had known him . . . yet it turned out he was one of the few people who had made up his mind about what was important to him and was confident enough to go ahead and just *be himself*.

Boy, she thought ruefully, if that's what being a "nerd" is, then just about everybody I know should try being more of a nerd! Including Christine Pratt!

The open way in which she and Peter were talking gave her confidence.

"There's something else I want to ask you, Peter. I'm just curious. Have you ever shown any of this to any of the *girls* you know?"

Peter chuckled. "There you go again, asking those funny questions. As a matter of fact, no, I haven't."

"Not even to your girlfriend?"

"Well . . . I don't have a girlfriend, Charlie."

"How come?"

Peter's cheeks were flushed as he shrugged and said, "I'm afraid most of the girls I know think of me as the school nerd or something."

Chris bit her lip.

"I guess I'll just have to wait until I'm older to find a girl who appreciates me. One who can see a boy for who he really is, not just how good-looking he is or what kind of car he has or how many teams he's the captain of."

Now it was Chris's turn to turn pink. "Is . . . is there any girl at Whittington High that you particularly like?"

Peter looked over at Charlie and grinned. "Well, sure. And here I thought it was as plain as the nose on my face. I think your cousin Chris is pretty terrific."

"Even though she's just as guilty as all the other girls you know? I mean, in terms of not being able to see boys for who they really are?"

"I'm not so sure that's true. I can't explain it, but I have this funny feeling about Christine Pratt. I think that even though she tries really hard to be popular at school and run around having a million dates and being a cheerleader and a competitive swimmer and everything else, underneath it all she's really a very caring, sensitive, understanding person. Someone who doesn't always have to go along with what everyone else is doing but who has the courage to figure out what's important to her and just *do* it."

If only he knew! Chris thought miserably. Peter

Blake believes I possess all these wonderful, positive qualities, when I've been acting just like all those superficial girls he just described! Especially where making assumptions about "the school nerd" is concerned!

"But I shouldn't be telling you all this," Peter teased. "After all, you *are* Chris's cousin. How do I know you won't run back to her house and tell her everything I've just said?"

"Oh, don't worry," Chris said, still feeling like a real heel. "Your secret is safe with me. I won't tell a soul."

"I trust you, Charlie. You seem like the kind of guy who's always honest. Who really means what he says. Who isn't afraid to show the world what he *really* is."

Inwardly, Chris groaned.

"I guess you and your cousin Chris are alike in that way," Peter went on. "You're both really sincere, trustworthy people."

This time, she was pleased by Peter's description.

Wait a minute, she thought all of a sudden. Why am I getting so concerned over what Peter thinks about Chris—I mean me?

The answer to that question was so obvious that she felt foolish for even having asked it of herself.

Eleven

"Why so glum, chum?"

Chris and Susan were lingering over breakfast on Thursday morning, both of them lost in their own daydreams as they toyed with their French toast long after their parents had gone on their way. Chris was thinking about the Marshmallow Masquerade—especially the things she still wanted to accomplish, now that Charlie Pratt had only two days left.

Susan, on the other hand, was thinking about something quite different.

"Hmmm?" she said dreamily, looking up from the smear of maple syrup on her plate that she had been distractedly running her spoon through.

"I said, why so glum, chum?" Chris repeated. "You look as if you've just lost your best friend."

Susan laughed half-heartedly. "Oh, I was just thinking about the Homecoming Dance, that's all."

Chris's eyebrows immediately went up. "Oh, really? I thought that the Homecoming Dance was supposed to be fun.''

"Oh, I suppose it is . . . if you've got a date.''

"Wait a minute," Chris demanded. "Is this the same girl who, only days ago, was claiming that she had absolutely no qualms about calling up a boy and asking him out?''

"I'm not going to ask anyone to the dance," said Susan. "It's not that I *wouldn't*, mind you. It's just that I have no idea whether the person I'd like to invite is the least bit interested in going with me." She sighed deeply. "How about you, Chris? Are you having any luck learning about Scott Stevens—and whether or not he might like to go to the dance with Charlie Pratt's cousin?''

Now it was Chris's turn to look serious. "It's funny, Sooz. A few days ago, I would have given anything to go to that dance with Scott. But ever since I've gotten to see the side of him that only his male friends would ordinarily get to see. . . .''

Susan grinned. "So he's not your Prince Charming after all, huh?''

"I'm not sure yet. But there's one thing you can count on.''

"What's that?''

"That Charlie Pratt's goal for day four of the Marshmallow Masquerade is to get to the bottom of this, once and for all. To find out whether or not Scott really is the boy for me. The Marshmallow Masquerade marches on!''

Even though Chris tried to sound light-hearted, she had to admit that she was feeling more confused than ever. Today, she intended to give Scott one more chance. To figure out how she really felt about him.

And to figure out how she really felt about Peter Blake.

There was something else she intended to do, as well. But that was something that had nothing to do with her, that was her way of saying "thank you" to her twin for thinking up the Marshmallow Masquerade.

"Yes," Chris said aloud, "I—I mean, *Charlie* has a lot to do today, so we'd better get rolling. Besides, that last piece of French toast of yours looks like it's had about all the handling it can stand!"

By now, playing the role of Charlie Pratt had become so predictable that it was almost routine. The students in Chris's class had gotten used to the "new boy," and many of them went out of their way to make him feel at home. She still couldn't get over how easily they had accepted the fact that he was a boy. . . . Although, she thought merrily, I have to give my acting skills *some* credit!

Even gym class was much easier the second time around.

"Hey, Charlie! It's good to see you again!" Peter Blake greeted Charlie as soon as Chris showed up in the gym, dressed in the same baggy shorts and oversized sweatshirt she'd worn on Tuesday.

"Same here," said Chris. "Listen, Peter, I really enjoyed coming over to your house yesterday. All those animals of yours are really something!"

"Gee, I'm glad you think so. And you're welcome to come back again, any time you want!" Suddenly, Peter's smile faded. "I almost forgot. You'll only be in Whittington until Saturday, right? That's too bad. . . ."

Chris wanted so much to be able to tell Peter that his

new friend wasn't *really* leaving, that the two of them could still get together. . . . But of course, she couldn't.

So instead, she said, "You know, Peter, my cousin Chris really likes animals, too. You should show her the 'Peter Blake Zoo' one of these days."

Peter began to blush. "Aw, I don't think she'd want to. . . ."

But before Charlie could insist that his cousin would indeed be pleased to come over to Peter's house, Mr. Nagle blew his whistle to signify that gym class was ready to begin.

Fortunately, the class spent the period trying out the gymnastic equipment once again. The tasks were a bit more difficult this time, but Chris had no trouble keeping up.

She couldn't help feeling somewhat self-conscious, though. After all, she had overheard Scott and his friends saying that Charlie Pratt was "puny." She was aware of Scott in particular as she tried a handstand on the parallel bars and performed all the other gymnastic feats along with the boys in the gym class.

Is it my imagination? she wondered over and over again. Or is Scott looking at me in a strange way?

Oh, no! Maybe he's figured it out! Maybe he knows I'm really Chris after all and not some make-believe cousin named Charlie.

She found out what was on his mind right after gym class was over. As she strolled over to the locker room, walking extra slowly so she'd be the last one in and could therefore slip into the boys' locker room to change without being noticed, Scott came over to her.

"You know, Charlie," he said, looking at her in that

same quizzical way, "there's something kind of . . . odd about you."

Uh-oh, thought Chris. Here goes. I'm about to be found out.

"What do you mean?" she asked, trying to sound calm.

"I don't understand you. I mean, how could you be friends with a guy like *me* . . . and also hang around with someone like Peter Blake?"

Chris was so relieved that Scott hadn't just declared that he knew that Charlie and Chris were one and the same person that it took her a few seconds to realize what he really had said. When she did, she suddenly became furious.

"What's wrong with that?"

"Oh, come on, Charlie," Scott said matter-of-factly. "Peter Blake is a *nerd*. Everybody knows that. He's no good at sports; he's a real zero with girls—"

"Really? Is that what you think?"

"Well, sure."

"Let me ask you something, Scott. What do you think—I mean, what do you *really* think—of my cousin Chris?"

"Chris Pratt?" Scott thought for a minute. "I'd say she's okay. She's pretty, she's popular, she's really involved with clubs and school sports. Oh, she's a cheerleader, too; that's a big plus. Yeah, I guess Chris is the kind of girl I might like to go out with sometime."

"Well, then, what would you think if I told you that Chris would never go out with you in a million years? And that as a matter of fact, she's *dying* to go out with Peter Blake?"

Chris didn't wait for an answer. She stomped off,

knowing that she had made her point but suspecting that someone like Scott was simply too dense to get it, anyway.

She was surprised to discover that she didn't care. Anything that Scott Stevens may have thought, said, or done had ceased to be of the slightest interest or importance to her.

What *really* surprised her, however, was the fact that she had meant what she had said. She really was dying to go out with Peter Blake.

Once she was alone, inside the boys' room, Chris started to giggle uncontrollably.

Well, Scott, perhaps I owe you a thank-you after all, she thought. If it hadn't been for you, I might never have realized that a boy like Peter Blake is worth a *dozen* of you!

For the rest of the day, Chris was in such a good mood that it was all she could do to keep from singing. She had finally sorted out her true feelings about Scott and about Peter . . . something she might never have been able to do without the help of Charlie Pratt.

But she still had one more important mission to carry out.

Right after school, she headed for the Andersons' house. Sure enough, just as she'd hoped, Mike Anderson was home. He was in the garage, covered with grease, repairing a bicycle.

"Hiya, Mike!" Chris-as-Charlie called.

Mike looked up from the tire he was intently fitting into the bicycle frame. "Hey, Charlie! Good to see you! I'm glad you dropped by!"

"Yeah, well, I'm afraid I can't stay too long." Chris shuffled her feet nervously as she noticed the basketball hoop hung on the front of the garage, right over her head.

"Does that mean you won't have time to shoot some baskets after all?"

"I'm afraid not."

"How about looking at that basketball scrapbook I told you about?"

"Not this time," said Chris.

"Gee, that's too bad."

Mike sounded genuinely disappointed. For a moment, Chris found herself wondering what on earth her twin *saw* in this boy. But then she remembered that Susan and Mike—if they ever *did* actually get together—probably wouldn't spend too much time talking about basketball. As with everyone else, the way Mike Anderson treated the boys he knew was very different from the way he treated the girls he knew.

"I just wanted to talk to you for a minute," Chris-as-Charlie went on. "You know, man to man."

"Sure, Charlie. What's on your mind?" Satisfied that the bike wheel was now firmly in place, Mike turned to face Charlie.

Chris realized then that while she had dropped in at the Andersons' solely for the purpose of getting Mike to ask Susan to the dance, she hadn't actually given much thought to *how* she would do it. From this moment on, she would simply have to play it by ear. Her mind was spinning with different tacts she could take.

And then, in a flash, she had an idea. She decided to rely on the buddy-buddy approach.

"Well, uh, I was wondering if you'd do me a favor, Mike."

"Sure, Charlie." Mike shrugged. "Anything. Just name it."

"This is kind of a lot to ask, but . . . my cousin Susan doesn't have a date for the Homecoming Dance this Saturday night. And I thought maybe you could . . . you know, invite her."

Mike looked surprised. "Gee, I'd be glad to help you out, pal. But do you think she'd really want to go with me?"

There it was again: that same insecurity about girls. Yet boys were always expected to be the ones to make the telephone calls, to set up the dates . . . to take all the risks by acting first. As in the case of so many things that Chris had thought about for the very first time throughout the week, it just didn't make any sense at all.

"Mike, let's just say I've got some inside information. I know for a fact that my cousin Sooz—I mean, Susan—would really like to go out with you."

Mike brightened. "Hey, great! I mean, uh, I'm glad I can help you out." He wiped his greasy hands on a rag. "Tell you what: I'll go give her a call right now." Before rushing into the house, however, he turned back for a moment. "Listen, Charlie, let me know if there's anything else I can do for you, okay?"

Chris was amused as she went on her way, whistling a light-hearted tune. There, that had been easy enough! As Chris, she never would have been able to approach Mike, almost a total stranger, and suggest that he ask a particular girl out. But as a fellow boy, there was no problem at all! In fact, Mike didn't even have to admit that he had been interested in Susan all along, as she now suspected was the case, given his eagerness to "do Charlie a favor."

117

Now, thought Chris, if I could only think of some-one to match up Beth Thompson with.

As she walked home, Chris's mind was racing as she tried to fit together all the pieces of all the things she had learned so far that week as Charlie Pratt. Why, she had had no idea that being a boy was so different from being a girl . . . and yet, at the same time, so alike in ways that never would have occurred to her before. She had seen sides of both Peter and Scott that she never would have seen as a girl. And she had managed to pull off a bit of matchmaking that Christine Pratt would have had quite a difficult time accomplishing!

Looking back on the week so far, Chris experienced a real sense of satisfaction. The Marshmallow Mas-querade was a success, not only because of the ease with which it had been carried off but also because of all she had been forced to think about, most of it for the very first time.

"Yes, Charlie Pratt," she said aloud, aware that she was talking to herself but certain that in this case it was completely justified, "no matter how the rest of the week turns out, one thing's for certain. You're the best friend any girl ever had!"

Twelve

Chris opened her eyes to bright sunlight streaming through her bedroom windows, the smell of breakfast wafting up the stairs . . . and a dull ache in the pit of her stomach. For a few seconds she lay in bed, puzzling over the way she felt.

Then she remembered. It was Friday.

Today was the last day of the Marshmallow Masquerade—and the day of Charlie Pratt's fight with Eddie McKay.

Chris wasn't the only one thinking about the day ahead. Even before she'd climbed out of bed, her twin poked her head in the doorway.

"Are you asleep?" Susan asked in a soft voice. She was still wearing her blue flannel nightgown.

Chris groaned loudly. "I wish I were. Then maybe all this would just be a bad dream."

"Oh, no. You're not still thinking about fighting with Eddie after school today, are you?"

"Sooz, I have to. We've come this far with the

Marshmallow Masquerade, and we can't give up now."

"But Chris—"

"We've already talked about this, and there's nothing left to discuss."

As if to demonstrate that she had no more to say about the matter, Chris bounded out of bed and began putting on her clothes. Her *Charlie* clothes.

While the rest of her family downed a hearty breakfast, Chris sat in front of an empty plate. She was having trouble swallowing even a glass of orange juice. The butterflies in her stomach simply refused to go away.

"Eat something, Chris," Susan pleaded. "At least have a piece of toast. After all, you need to keep your strength up."

Mr. Pratt perked up immediately. "Oh, really? What's up? Have you got something exciting planned for day five of this Marshmallow Masquerade of yours?"

"Oh, no," Chris assured him quickly. "Nothing out of the ordinary. Just the same old thing."

Susan cast her a wary glance.

"It's just that today's the last day. First thing tomorrow morning, Charlie Pratt goes back to Chicago, never to be seen or heard from again."

"That is, if he makes it to tomorrow morning," Susan muttered.

Underneath the table, Chris gave her a light kick.

"Well, I'm going to miss old Charlie," Mr. Pratt said cheerfully.

"Not me," said Susan a bit woefully. "Frankly, I'm looking forward to getting Chris back. She was always so . . . so level-headed. So realistic. So *smart*."

Chris just made a face.

All that day, however, she could think of little besides her inevitable confrontation with Eddie McKay. Especially after what happened in homeroom.

"Hey, Charlie Pratt," Eddie said with a sneer as soon as he saw Chris-as-Charlie slink into the classroom. "You know that expression 'Thank God It's Friday'? Well, after today, it'll have new meaning for you!"

Predictably, Frank and Jimmy laughed loudly. Chris just glared at the three of them, then sat down and buried her face in one of her notebooks.

But the truth of the matter was, she was scared.

While she had lifted weights and done push-ups all week, she was no more confident about her ability to take on Eddie McKay in a fist fight than she had been on Monday. All morning she had trouble listening in class. She was too busy trying to remember the moves she had seen in every fight she'd ever seen, in movies and on television.

And then, as the last period of the day rolled around and her fight with Eddie was less than an hour away, she realized a very fundamental fact.

She had been concentrating on using her muscles when she should have been concentrating on using her brain.

When the final bell of the day rang and the halls of Whittington High filled up with students hurrying to get to their lockers and dash out of the school building so that their weekend could begin, Chris still had butterflies in her stomach. And she was still scared. But for the first time all week, she was convinced that she—or, rather, Charlie Pratt—could deal with Eddie McKay.

She waited for him in the schoolyard. Sure enough, within ten minutes of the last bell, he came sashaying out of the school building, with Jimmy and Frank a few feet behind. She was surprised to see that other students—mostly boys, many of them Eddie's friends—were heading over in the same direction, as well. Apparently word about the fight between the school bully and the new boy had spread, and a crowd of spectators was about to gather.

"So, Pratt," said Charlie in his usual menacing tone as he swaggered toward her, "I hope you're ready to settle this once and for all. I hope you're ready to fight!"

At least two dozen students had formed a loose circle around Eddie and Charlie, who were standing face to face. Eddie was hunched over, his eyes narrowed, his hands clenched into fists. There was silence all around, and so much tension in the air that it was almost like a fog.

But Charlie Pratt was relaxed. He stood very still, with his hands stuck deep inside his jacket pockets. There was a funny half-smile on his face.

"Eddie," he finally said, "I have no intention of fighting with you."

"Oh, yeah?" the school bully countered. "What are you, scared?"

"That's not really the point."

"Hah, you're scared! You're a *coward*, Charlie Pratt! Coward! Coward!"

Charlie looked Eddie in the eye and shrugged. "If that's what you call somebody who walks away from a fight, if a 'coward' is your name for someone who'd rather not get a black eye or a bloody nose, given the choice, then, yes, I'm a coward."

Eddie snorted. But it was obvious that this unexpected turn of events had him bewildered. "Don't you care that everybody around school—everybody in the whole *town*, in fact—is going to be saying you're chicken?"

"Eddie," Charlie said calmly, "for the rest of my life, whatever I do, there are always going to be people who don't like it. People who call me silly names or make fun of me or just think I'm making mistakes. But do you want to know something, Eddie? I don't care. I don't care because I've got to live my life the way *I* decide to live it. It's not important for me to try to please anybody but myself."

"You're . . . you're just saying all this because . . . because you're scared to fight," Eddie stuttered. He was trying to sound gruff, but instead, he just sounded baffled.

Charlie laughed. "Eddie, I'd like to meet the person who's *not* afraid to fight! Let's just say I've decided not to, because I don't think there's anything important enough to fight over. Or anything that can really be accomplished by fighting. So let's leave it at that, okay?"

"Oh, yeah? Well, what would you do if I came over and punched you in the stomach right now?"

"I'd probably fall down. And it would probably hurt a lot. But to tell you the truth, I don't think you'd do that."

"Yeah? How come?"

"Because you're basically an intelligent, reasonable guy, that's why." Chris-as-Charlie extended her hand. Her chin was held high, and her brown eyes were locked steadily in Eddie's. "So how about if you and I try being friends, instead?"

There was total silence in the schoolyard for almost half a minute. Both Eddie's friends and Charlie Pratt's newfound allies were standing perfectly still, holding their breath, waiting to see what was going to happen.

And then, all of a sudden, Eddie turned around and started walking out of the schoolyard.

"Friends, hah!" he called over his shoulder. "Eddie McKay doesn't have cowards as friends!"

As she watched him strut away, with Frank and Jimmy scampering after him, Chris suddenly felt weak in the knees. And she realized for the first time that she was shaking. But before she had a chance to think about what *could* have happened, she felt a friendly hand on her shoulder.

"Not bad, Charlie! Not bad at all!"

Chris turned and found herself face to face with Scott Stevens.

"Hey, you look pretty shaken up. You're all red." Scott sounded concerned.

"Well, confronting the school bully isn't exactly the *easiest* thing in the world!"

Scott chuckled. "You deserve congratulations—and a big thank-you from everybody at Whittington High. Eddie McKay has been making trouble around here for as long as I can remember. He needed somebody to stand up to him once and for all. I guess it took an outsider to do it."

Chris was suddenly modest. "Aw, it was nothing, really."

Especially considering that I had nothing to lose! she thought ruefully.

But Scott wasn't about to take Charlie Pratt's triumph lightly. "Are you kidding? You proved you were a man today! Even more than if you'd fought with Eddie! Boy, you've really got a lot of guts!"

Chris opened her mouth to say something about Scott's definition of "manhood" when she noticed her twin sister running toward her across the schoolyard.

"Excuse me a minute, Scott," said Chris. "Here comes Susan, my, uh, cousin. I'd like to talk to her alone for a minute."

"Oh, sure." Instead of going on his way, however, Scott just moved away a few feet, as if he were waiting for Charlie.

"Are you all right?" Susan demanded once she reached her twin. "You look okay. . . ."

"I'm fine," Chris reassured her. "I didn't fight."

"Oh, Chris! I'm so glad you changed your mind! I was so scared . . . I couldn't even bring myself to watch. I figured if I waited a few minutes, I'd be able to help you get home without having had to watch you and Eddie punch it out.

"But fortunately, it seems you two didn't actually fight. What happened?"

"Well, Sooz, you know that I was determined to do this thing right. That I wanted to do everything that I would do if I really were a boy, in order to make the Marshmallow Masquerade real, instead of just some game."

"I'll say. Even though I thought you were taking things just a bit too far. . . ."

"But I realized today that even if I *were* really a boy, I wouldn't have fought with Eddie. It's wrong, and that's all there is to it. Sure, boys are expected to fight. But people don't always have to do what's *expected* of them, do they? Especially if it's just because they happen to be a boy . . . or a girl. And

125

doubly especially if it goes against what they believe is right."

Chris shrugged, then continued. "Somewhere along the line, all of us—boys *and* girls—have to decide what we want to do, what's important to us, what we feel is right. And we have to stick to it, no matter what anybody else says. No matter what all the other boys, or all the other girls, are doing. No matter what people are always saying that boys or girls are 'supposed' to do. There are no real rules about what it means to be a boy or to be a girl; only myths and fairy tales that people have made up over the years. We're all different, and we're all individuals. And we've all got to start living that way!"

All of a sudden, Sooz leaned over and gave her sister a big hug.

"What's that for?" Chris asked, surprised.

"I'm so proud of you, Chris," her twin whispered. "And I'm so pleased that we've both learned so much from the Marshmallow Masquerade—and from Charlie Pratt!"

Chris grinned. "Unfortunately, I don't think Eddie McKay has learned a *thing* from Charlie!"

"Hey, Charlie," Scott called impatiently, "how about going over to Fozzy's for some ice cream? You, too, Susan. I'll even treat, just to show you what a nice guy I am."

Susan looked at her twin with merriment in her eyes. Chris knew what she was thinking, that the idea of going to Fozzy's with Scott Stevens was undoubtedly the ultimate for Chris.

So Susan was amazed when Chris said, "Thanks, Scott, but there's something else I've got to do right now."

Scott just shrugged. "Okay, Charlie. Suit yourself. I'll see you around!" And he was off.

Susan, however, was too curious to let Chris get away without giving her an explanation. "Am I missing something here? As I recall, just a few days ago my twin sister would have given her entire record collection just for the chance to sit next to the captain of Whittington High's basketball team!"

"Let's just say that the Marshmallow Masquerade gave me an inside look at Scott Stevens. That Charlie Pratt saw a side of him that Chris Pratt may well have never gotten to see. And to tell you the truth, I wasn't exactly thrilled with what I saw."

"So it turns out that Scott isn't for you," said Susan with a sigh. "That's too bad. Especially since the Homecoming Dance is tomorrow night, and it's always so nice to go to something like that with someone special."

"Oh, don't worry," Chris said with a twinkle in her eye. "If things turn out the way I'm hoping they will, I'll be going to that dance with someone *very* special!"

Susan was puzzled. "I don't understand. Has someone new stolen my twin sister's heart without me knowing about it?"

"Sort of," Chris laughed. "Yes, he's stolen my heart. But he's not someone new. And the real surprise is that he's someone you'd probably never expect me to fall for, not in a million years."

"Uh-oh," Susan teased. "Sounds like the work of Charlie Pratt once again. Letting you see sides of the boys you've known for years . . . I mean, the boys you *thought* you knew for years!"

"Something like that."

127

"And has this mystery man asked you to that dance?"

"No, not exactly."

"Well, then, how exactly do you plan to arrange this little date of yours?"

Chris pretended to be astonished. "Why, Susan Pratt! You're the one who gave me the idea in the first place! It was during one of your little speeches about the differences between boys and girls, as I recall . . . that is, about the *ridiculous* differences, which aren't really differences at all."

Susan's brown eyes narrowed. "Christine Pratt, what are you up to now?"

"Oh, nothing." Chris took her sister's arm and began leading her out of the schoolyard. "But we'd better get going. Christine Pratt has suddenly experienced a miracle cure. Her flu is gone; she's feeling terrific. She can't wait to go to the Homecoming Dance . . . and she has to hurry up and make a very important phone call to a very important person."

Thirteen

On Saturday night, the night of Whittington High's Homecoming Dance, Chris was dressed and ready to go by seven o'clock. She was wearing her new pale blue dress, her short hair was freshly washed and brushed back in an attractive feathery style, and she had chosen just the right jewelry to set off her outfit: simple gold earrings and a gold heart locket. At that hour, however, her twin sister was nowhere to be found.

"Where on earth is Susan?" Chris wondered aloud as she opened up a big bag of potato chips and emptied it into a serving dish. She and her mother were in the kitchen, getting things ready for the little pre-dance get-together that the twins had, at the last minute, decided to throw. The plan was that four couples would meet at the Pratts' house, have a snack, and then all set off for the Homecoming Dance together.

The first guests were expected at any minute . . .

yet Susan still hadn't returned from the mysterious "errand" she'd set out on, immediately after dinner.

"I'm starting to get worried," Chris went on. "Beth and Holly and the others should be here soon. Besides, Sooz still has to get dressed for the dance. It's so late. Where do you suppose she went?"

"I don't know, but it looks as if you'll be finding out in about thirty seconds," said Mrs. Pratt, peering out the kitchen window. "She just pulled up in the driveway."

Sure enough, a short while later Susan came bustling into the kitchen. Even though she was bundled up in mittens, a wool scarf, and a knitted ski cap with a pompom pulled way down over her ears, her cheeks were flushed pink from the cold November evening.

"Susan Pratt, where *were* you?" Chris demanded, looking up from the bowl of onion dip she was mixing with a wooden spoon. "Everyone will be here any minute, and you still have to get dressed."

"Yes," said Mrs. Pratt. "Your sister here was getting quite concerned. She was afraid she might have to host this little party without you!"

"Sorry," Susan said with a wide grin. "My 'errand' took a little bit longer than I expected."

"I can't imagine what was so important that it couldn't wait. You'd better hurry."

"Don't worry, Chris. All I have to do is put on my dress and I'll be all set." She pulled off her mittens and stuck them in the pockets of her jacket.

Chris stopped what she was doing and faced her twin. She was still holding on to her wooden spoon. "What about your hair? Aren't you going to wash it or at least do something special with it for the dance?"

"Funny you should mention that," Susan said. There was a mischievous twinkle in her dark brown eyes. "As a matter of fact, I *did* do something special with my hair for the dance."

With that, she pulled off her knitted cap—and revealed the same short haircut that her sister had gotten, exactly one week before, in honor of the Marshmallow Masquerade.

"Sooz!" Chris squealed, dropping her spoon onto the kitchen floor. "You've cut off all your hair!"

"Yes, I have," Susan said matter-of-factly. "And now you and I are identical twins again!"

She reached up to touch the short haircut, as if she wasn't yet used to it—the same way her sister had reacted when she first had hers cut. Unlike Chris's, however, Susan's was brushed back into an attractive style right from the start. "We can let it grow together. And in the meantime, we'll be ready for any practical jokes that may come along that require two pranksters who happen to look exactly the same!"

"Oh, Sooz, that's great!" Chris leaned over and gave her sister a big hug. "And you look terrific, if I do say so myself."

"And here I was just getting used to being able to tell the two of you apart," said Mrs. Pratt with a sigh. "Now I'll have to go back to second-guessing you, trying to figure out which one of you is Chris and which one is Susan!"

"Sorry, Mom," Susan laughed. "Now, if you two will excuse me, I'd better run upstairs and get dressed. I've got a dance to go to!"

As Susan was trotting upstairs to her bedroom, the doorbell rang.

"Oh, dear!" Chris wailed. "They're here—already! And I'm not done yet."

"That's all right, Chris. I'll take over," Mrs. Pratt offered. "Why don't you go greet your guests? I'll finish up in here."

"Yum—and I'll help you," Mr. Pratt boomed as he came into the kitchen. "I can see you've got a lot of food to get rid of, and making a dent in it is the least I can do. I'll start off with these potato chips and this onion dip."

"Oh, Daddy!" Chris laughed. "Just make sure you leave one or two potato chips for the rest of us! After all, we'll all be needing our energy. We've got a long night of dancing ahead of us!" She dashed out of the kitchen, heading for the front door.

She was pleased to see that her date for the evening was the very first guest to arrive.

"Hello, Peter," Chris said with a welcoming smile.

"Hi, Chris," Peter said shyly. He was still astounded that the popular, outgoing Christine Pratt had called him up the day before and invited him to the Homecoming Dance. But even greater than his surprise was his extreme pleasure. "You certainly look nice this evening!"

"Thank you, Peter. You look nice, too!"

Peter looked a bit taken aback by her compliment. But Chris had surmised during Charlie Pratt's visit that boys needed to be complimented on their appearance, just as girls did. After all, it seemed only fair.

"Well, come on into the dining room. I'd like you to meet my parents. And we've got some soda and some chips and other things to eat. Just help yourself!"

"Thanks." Peter followed Chris into the dining

room. "By the way, Chris, I, uh, just wanted to tell you how great I think it is that you called me and asked me out. I mean, that probably wasn't a very easy thing for a girl to do."

Chris shrugged. "Not any harder than it would be for a boy to do. Besides," she added teasingly, "I had a pretty good idea that if I asked you to the dance, it was fairly certain that you'd say yes."

"Oh, no! Don't tell me Charlie told you something. . . ."

"Charlie didn't say a word to me before he left this morning, not about you or about anything else."

Peter grinned. "Yeah, I had a feeling about Charlie all along. That he was trustworthy, I mean. He's okay, that cousin of yours. As a matter of fact, I'm really going to miss him."

"I know what you mean," Chris agreed heartily. "Charlie's visit is something that none of us will forget for a very long time!"

When the doorbell rang a second time, Susan came racing down the stairs, dressed up in a pretty yellow dress, yelling, "I'll get it!"

Just as she'd hoped, it was her date for the evening.

"Hi, Mike," she greeted the tall blond boy standing in the doorway.

"Hi, Susan! All ready to dance the night away?"

"I certainly am! That is, after I've finished stuffing myself full of potato chips." Like Peter, Susan was still surprised by the dance invitation she'd gotten, only two days earlier. She couldn't have been happier about it, of course. Even so, she couldn't help wondering if her "cousin" Charlie had had anything to do with matching up her and Mike.

"Come on in, Mike, and have something to eat. My

mother and Chris have been in the kitchen for over an hour, concocting all kinds of goodies."

"Okay, thanks. Hey, by the way, your hair looks terrific! I like it short."

"Oh, really? I'm so glad. I just had it cut today." Susan smoothed out her new short style. "There's something to be said for short hair. It's so easy to take care of, for one thing."

"I know," Mike agreed with a chuckle. "That's something we boys have known about for years!"

It wasn't long before the other two couples arrived: Holly and Hank, looking quite comfortable with each other and happy over being reunited, and Beth and Dennis, two quiet people who were just getting to know each other—but were obviously quite pleased to be having such an opportunity.

Finally, all eight of them were assembled in the dining room, joking and laughing and attacking the food with such enthusiasm that it was difficult to believe that only about an hour earlier each of them had been eating dinner.

"Well, I guess we have Chris and Mrs. Pratt to thank for this little get-together," said Mike, dropping ice cubes into a glass full of root beer.

"Oh, I don't know about that," Chris said modestly. "If we have anyone to thank, I'd have to say it's Charlie Pratt. You know, our cousin from Chicago."

"Ah, yes," Susan agreed with a knowing smile. "It's true that he turned out to be quite a matchmaker, didn't he?"

Shyly, Chris looked at Peter, Mike looked at Sooz, Hank looked at Holly, and Dennis looked at Beth—all of them assuming that they, and they alone, were the people to whom Susan was referring when she mentioned Charlie Pratt's role as a matchmaker.

"It's just too bad he couldn't have stuck around a little longer," Hank commented. "Maybe come to the dance tonight."

"Yes, it is too bad," Beth agreed. "I'm afraid I never even got a chance to meet him."

"Well," said Peter hopefully, "maybe he'll come back to visit again sometime soon. What do you think, Chris?"

Chris and Susan looked at each other and grinned.

"Maybe he will, one of these days" was all that Chris said.

"Don't forget," Susan added, her eyes on her twin, "that Charlie contributed a lot more than improving everyone's social life. Just having him around was a real education."

"I'll say," Chris returned. "I suspect that after only a week with Charlie around, Susan and I will never look at things in quite the same way again!"

After almost all the food was gone and Mr. Pratt had dutifully snapped photographs of all of them, the four couples decided it was time to be on their way.

"After all," said Mike, smiling warmly at Susan as he helped her with her coat, "we don't want to miss any of the Homecoming Dance. This is a pretty special occasion!"

"It's a *very* special occasion," Susan agreed. "This is a special night for all of us, and I want to make sure I enjoy every single moment of it." With that, she reached for Mike's coat and started to help him put it on. "Here, let me help you with that," she insisted.

Mike hesitated for a moment, surprised by her offer.

But then he broke out into a huge grin. "Well, sure! Why not? I suppose I appreciate the little courtesies of life just as much as the female half of the population does!"

"I hope you feel that way, too," Chris said, turning to Peter.

"Sure I do!" he said. "I've always believed that *all* people, both male and female, deserve the same courtesies. The way I look at it, we're not that different, are we?"

It was all that Chris could do to keep from bursting out laughing. And as she looked over at her twin, she saw that Susan was having the same difficulty.

"No, Peter, I guess we're not."

Chris reached for his jacket and held it out, at arm's length. "Here, let me help you put on your coat. After all," she explained, exchanging a secret smile with her sister, "I have a feeling that Charlie Pratt would have wanted it this way!"

About the Author

Cynthia Blair first decided to become a writer when she was six years old, but it was twenty years before she realized that dream. She grew up on Long Island, earned her B.A. from Bryn Mawr College in Pennsylvania, and went on to get an M.S. in business from M.I.T. In fact, it was while she was supposed to be working on her thesis that she started her first novel. After four years of writing while working as a marketing manager for food companies, she abandoned the corporate life in order to concentrate full-time on her novels.

Ms. Blair lives in Manhattan with her husband, Richard, and her son, Jesse.

TAF-75

By the year 2000, 2 out of 3 Americans could be illiterate.

It's true.

Today, 75 million adults...about one American in three, can't read adequately. And by the year 2000, U.S. News & World Report envisions an America with a literacy rate of only 30%.

Before that America comes to be, you can stop it...by joining the fight against illiteracy today.

Call the Coalition for Literacy at toll-free **1-800-228-8813** and volunteer.

**Volunteer
Against Illiteracy.
The only degree you need
is a degree of caring.**

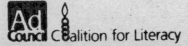

Ad Council   Coalition for Literacy   LV-2